Stranger at the Crossroads

Gena Dalton

Love Inspired®

Published by Steeple Hill Books™

STEEPLE HILL BOOKS

ISBN 0-373-87181-3

STRANGER AT THE CROSSROADS

Visit us at www.steeplehill.com

Printed in U.S.A.

But a Samaritan traveler who came upon him was moved with compassion when he saw him. He went up and bandaged his wounds, pouring oil and wine on them. He then lifted him on to his own mount, carried him to the inn and looked after him.

—*Luke* 10:33-34

This story is dedicated to God, Who, as always, gave me the book, and to my friends Karen and Paula, who helped me listen for the words. I would also like to thank my friend Jill Peale, DVM, who advised me on all matters veterinary. Any mistakes are mine alone.

Chapter One

Stealing a horse wasn't easy. At least not this one.

Jackson McMahan put the halter and lead rope behind his back and tried to soothe the mare with his voice while he slowly moved closer to her.

"Settle down, now, girl," he crooned, "I'm not gonna hurt you."

Finally, ten or fifteen minutes after he'd driven onto Blake Collier's ranch by the back road so he wouldn't have to pass the house, he maneuvered the nervous animal into a corner. He shifted off his good leg onto his lame one and, ignoring the sudden pain in his knee that made his gait even more awkward, stepped up to her head without spooking her.

Her big belly slowed her down, and too little food had made her weak, so he managed to get his arm around her neck, and then the rope, just before she tried to break away again. He let out a sigh of relief that he hadn't known he was holding.

"Come on home with me, Mama, and get a square meal," he said, while he slipped the halter onto her head and buckled it with his clumsy gloved hands. "You want your baby to have all its parts, don't you?"

It was way too late to affect that, though, he decided, glancing over his shoulder as he led her out of the pen and toward the trailer's open door. From the looks of her distended sides with the ribs standing out under her skin, this foal would be on the ground, alive or dead, before it had a chance to absorb very many days' worth of nutrients.

He had brought the three-horse trailer with the ramp so she wouldn't have to make the short leap up into it, but that didn't help much. She refused to have anything to do with the trailer. She balked and pawed the ground and swung side to side every time he tried to lead her forward.

Jackson glanced over his shoulder toward the house. No sign of life.

That was good, because Blake Collier would be much more likely to shoot a horse thief than to call the sheriff.

He smooched to the mare again, waited, and smooched again. When she took a tiny step forward, he started up the ramp as if he thought that was what she'd intended to do. Suddenly docile, she walked beside him. He led her into a slot, ran the rope through the ring and, willing his fingers not to fumble too much, tied her off. His heart lifted as he fastened the divider and hurried to close the door and raise the ramp.

Shooting danger aside, any fight with Blake would be a toss-up now that Jackson's body was so unreliable—and an unnecessary delay, to boot. It was past time to get out of here.

Darcy Hart didn't recognize herself when she glanced in the rearview mirror. Wild green eyes stared back at her, unseeing, and her auburn curls whipped and tangled madly in the wind. She looked like an Orphan Annie doll scared half to death.

She didn't care. She had to have the fresh air. With the window rolled up, she couldn't even breathe.

It was almost cool this morning, with a nice October breeze blowing, but her cheeks felt burning hot. Well, then, they'd really feel hot in Mexico.

If she wound up in Mexico.

The sound and the rhythm of the tires against the pavement soothed her a little. She wouldn't have to stop again for awhile, since she'd filled the truck with gasoline before she stopped at last night's motel. She had no desire to eat, either.

Being on the move helped. It helped a lot. The dreams that had wakened her at 3:00 a.m. were fading again. Every mile seemed to put them farther away.

Not the sorrow, though. It was part of her now, as

much as her stomach and her veins and her fingers and toes, since it filled them all with its cold cement.

She prayed her constant and only prayer.

Dear God, please give me the strength to bear it.

Then she added a postscript.

You can see by where I am this morning that I don't have enough. More strength, Lord. More strength.

Never did she dare to pray for the sorrow to be taken away—then she would truly be alone.

The truck swerved on a narrow curve, and she set her gaze on the road again. She'd better be trying to hold it between the ditches if she didn't want to end up in one.

Actually, she didn't much care. Her life still wasn't worth living. It had been a year. A year that had been a hundred times longer without her dear, dear Todd to hold her in his arms every night and her precious baby boy, Daniel, with his huge dark eyes to gaze into with her own.

Grief rushed into her heart, fresh as ever.

Time heals, they'd all told her. You'll start looking to the future one of these days. Well, at this rate, since she'd made precious little progress in a year, she'd have to be the oldest woman on the planet before she lost even a little of her longing for the past. To get to that point, God would have to give her all His own strength.

At that instant, a cross appeared in the heavens.

Up ahead, on the right. A white cross shining in the sun against the blue morning sky.

Darcy stared, not caring that the truck swerved into the opposite lane. Her eyes were glued to that cross. Could it be a visible answer to her prayer?

She blinked and looked again as she straightened her steering. No, the cross wasn't floating in the sky. It rested atop an adobe building that vaguely reminded her of the Alamo. Ancient and small and run-down, it must be a church, or maybe even a private chapel, judging by the size. No miracles today.

Something flashed in the corner of her eye, something closer. A glint of silver, then she saw the shape of the horse trailer, and her focus came back to earth.

No one with a grain of sense would pull onto the side of a two-lane road with no shoulder like this one unless there was trouble. That spot was steep enough to tilt the trailer sideways.

The ramp was down, and the trailer door hung open, swaying a little over the deep ditch.

Maybe the driver was just checking on a horse that had been kicking the side or putting hay in the hay bag that he'd forgotten. It probably wasn't an emergency at all. At least, not a medical one.

She prepared to pull over to give a wider berth as she drew closer to the rig.

It was a blowout on a trailer tire. The trailer sat tilted sideways not just because of the terrain. One wheel rested on the ground because the tire had disintegrated. Darcy glimpsed pieces of rubber scattered over the road, but she couldn't look at anything but that open door. Was the horse hurt?

It surged into view at that moment, backing up fast and in a zigzag line. A man appeared, holding the lead rope, struggling to keep it from being jerked out of his hands, fighting to stay with the terrified animal as it plunged down the ramp.

A pregnant mare. Very pregnant. As she hit the ground with her hind feet, she lost purchase on the blacktop pavement and, scrabbling, half rearing, she slipped off the edge of the ditch and kept on sliding down the incline, reaching with her front legs for balance in the air.

The man held onto her, but it couldn't have been easy. He had something badly wrong with one leg and could barely keep on his feet and stay with the desperate mare. She reared mightily as the fear rushed through her, hauling the rope through his gloved hands so fast that he came within a heartbeat of losing it. He had all he could do to stay out from under her raised forefeet, but he did it. Darcy pulled even with them.

The mare was huge with the foal that had obviously sapped every bit of her resources. It was a miracle she even had the strength to rush out of the trailer and try to get away, much less fight to stay out of the ditch. The red dun mare had spirit, that was for sure.

She wasn't hurt, though. She didn't appear to be hurt.

"Don't stop," Darcy said to herself out loud. "Do. Not. Stop."

She stopped.

The trembling, sweating mare, her eyes rolling into the whites, stretched impossibly higher against the early morning sky, then threw herself backward into the bottom of the ditch.

"Hang on," Darcy called, through the open passenger window. "I'll help you."

She pulled off the road in front of the man's new Ford dually, killed the engine, leaped out and ran to him and the mare. He whirled on his heel and glared at her. He was furious. Absolutely furious.

And handsome as any man she'd ever seen. He had a strange intensity about him that held her eye, and it wasn't just the anger. Blue eyes like flames in a fire and black hair. Weathered and tanned face, chiseled and lined some from wind and sun, but she doubted he was more than thirty-five.

Why was she even noticing anything about him? She'd stopped because of the horse.

"Get back on the road," he said, before she'd reached him. "Get out of here."

He barked the order in a tone hateful enough to drive anyone away. Anyone who cared.

"I'd love nothing more," Darcy said.

It was true. She couldn't handle her own affairs, and here she was meddling in somebody else's. She didn't want to be around anyone, especially not such a venomous someone, because what she wanted, what she *needed,* was to be alone to think about her own problems.

Stopping had been a stupid thing to do when she was supposed to be running away—from her profession as well as from the rest of her life. She looked into the ditch.

The little red dun was wedged on her left side in the narrow space, struggling to find her feet but unable to get up or even move her legs much at all. She was cast. It'd be impossible for her to get her feet under her and get up without help.

It wouldn't be long, either, until the mare ran out of strength to help them help her.

Darcy heaved a huge sigh. She *had* taken an oath, after all.

"We've got to get her out of there pretty quick. I'll help you. I'm Dr. Darcy Hart. I'm a veterinarian."

"I saw the vet box," he snapped.

"So," she said, just as sharply. "Be grateful I happened along."

"Go back to Oklahoma."

"You're pretty observant for a man with a sick, cast horse in a ditch on the side of the road."

"It's hard not to notice a bossy woman veterinarian hollering orders at a perfect stranger."

Darcy felt a stab of anger.

"Hang on?" she said sarcastically. "I'll help you? That's all I said. You call *that* hollering orders?"

He pulled his straw hat down and impaled her with his bright blue gaze.

"Get on down the road," he said harshly. "I don't need any pity assistance."

She had to think about it, because she wasn't quite sure what he meant, at first. Then she knew. His leg. He thought she'd stopped because he was physically disabled.

Darcy looked him straight in the eye for another long beat. He wasn't the kind of man to seek or accept help from a woman. He was, no doubt, a typical male of the cowboy kind. Those men had the desire and duty and determination to protect and take care of any female bred right into their bones.

"I wouldn't waste my pity on you, mister," she said evenly, "although you deserve a truckload of it for being mean as a snake. My only concern here is the mare and foal."

He tried to hide it, but she saw a flash of surprise in his blazing eyes. And maybe…even a twitch of humorous appreciation at the corner of his mouth?

That gave her a tiny satisfaction.

Her blood was pulsing with urgency to help the mare, but she waited. He needed to decide what to do. He needed to be the one to give the orders if they weren't going to waste any more time arguing.

He was the kind of man she thought he was. He was a horseman, and the horse came first.

"I'll get a rope," he said. "Scoot down in there by her head and see if you can calm her a little."

Darcy started down into the ditch as he turned to his trailer.

"What's her name?" she called.

"Tara."

"What's yours?"

He hesitated for an instant, as if she had a lot of nerve to ask, but finally he answered.

"Jackson."

Whether that was his first name or his last, Darcy couldn't tell. But what did she care? It didn't matter. He wasn't the reason she was here.

Tara had stopped struggling for the moment, but her eyes were still showing fear, and she was looking over her shoulder at her flank. Darcy slid down the incline to her head and began stroking it and talking to her.

It helped a little. She struggled once again, hard, and then stopped.

Her breathing sounded wheezy, and it wasn't just from the fall. Since her eyes and nose were runny, there was every likelihood that the stress of the developing foal on such short rations had probably lowered her immune system and caused her to contract a respiratory virus.

Darcy's heart clutched as she sat on her haunches there, stroking the pretty head, looking into one of the big soft eyes of the mare. The foal would most likely be sickly, too, if it wasn't stillborn.

Jackson came back with a length of soft rope in his hands and managed, a bit precariously, to half-walk, half-slide into the ditch behind Tara. He talked to her soothingly so she'd know he was there and stepped sideways along the near side of it to reach her, all the while forming a loop in the rope with his gloved hands. Darcy thought vaguely that that would be easier to do without gloves.

Quickly, almost before she knew it, he had the rope around all four of Tara's feet and was making his way around her to the lower side of the ditch. He had a little trouble with the terrain, but he made it, and as Darcy got to her feet, ready to help, he set his heels into the ground as best he could, braced himself and pulled. Talking to the mare in a surprisingly soothing voice, he quickly pulled her feet over her massive belly so that she could stand.

"*I'll* get it," he said hatefully, hurrying around to take the rope off.

"All *right.*"

When he had it off, Darcy backed up to give Tara some room and pulled up on the lead rope to help her. Jackson gave her hindquarters a little help. Heavily, awkwardly, the mare got to her feet.

"Now," Darcy said, "let's get her out of the ditch and I'll look her over...."

"No need of that," he said, and he came past the mare to take the lead from her.

"Don't be ridiculous," Darcy snapped.

She tried to think, tried to control the sudden anger that took her. Here he had a volunteer veterinarian for a horse in danger and he wasn't even going to let her take care of the animal. How could he be such an ungrateful wretch?

The question stopped her short. The man didn't matter. The mare did.

She put a conscious effort into trying to control her temper. He had every right to send her away, and if she wanted this mare to have care, she had to get his permission.

"Jackson, you're a good horseman, I can tell," she said. "And this clearly is a good horse, even if she does look as if she's been turned out during a seven-year drought."

Jackson didn't answer. He led Tara out of the ditch and onto the side of the road.

Darcy followed.

"When you had the blowout, did you call anyone to come get her? She needs…"

"I had just had the blowout when you came along."

His tone said that was the end of the conversation.

"Well, while you wait for someone to come for her, let me check her…"

"I'll walk her home," he said harshly. "That's my barn over there."

He gestured toward a small barn and house that she hadn't noticed in the near distance, not far past the chapel. The place was within easy walking distance across a pasture.

The mare could make it that far, and Darcy could meet them there. If she could get him to agree.

A thought struck her. Maybe his infuriating attitude stemmed from worries about money. Yet his truck was expensive and new. His place wasn't, though.

"This is a new experience for me," she said. "Most of the time, people are trying to get free veterinary care instead of turning it down."

Still wheezing, Tara looked at her flanks as they walked toward the trailer, then lifted her head and looked straight at Darcy as if she knew she was trying to help her. Her tail lifted and switched back and forth restlessly. She was obviously in early labor and ready to foal.

Darcy patted her sweaty side and tried again.

"If you want her to get through this foaling alive, she's going to need some help."

Then it hit her.

"You don't want a *woman* veterinarian, do you? You're that narrow-minded!"

She bit her tongue. This was no way to get him to let her treat the mare.

It made him talk, though.

"I don't know why women are always trying to be equine vets when they're not strong enough to do half of what needs to be done," he said bitterly.

His blue eyes blazed at her again.

"And you're smaller than most."

"And you're more two-faced than most," she said, blazing back at him. "You act like a real horseman, yet you starve a fine mare. And then you deny her medical care.''

Jackson opened the tack room door of the trailer. He flicked a careless glance at her as if her opinion meant absolutely nothing to him.

''If you want a job so bad,'' he said, ''hold her a minute while I get a better halter.''

He handed Darcy the lead rope, opened the door and stepped into the neatly arranged tack room. Its contents included several expensive saddles on built-in racks. He could certainly afford a veterinarian.

Tara moved around uneasily, and Darcy turned her attention to the mare. Her tail was going like a metronome, switching back and forth. Back and forth. Then she dropped her head and seemed to be looking for a spot to lie down.

Dear Lord, don't let this mare foal right here in the road.

She was so angry with this strange, contradictory man she could scream. But she had to control her temper and her tongue or she'd never be able to help this good mare through her hard time coming.

Maybe she could be friendlier and accomplish more.

To calm herself and Tara, she stroked the horse's cheek some more. Her fingernail caught in one of the ravelings of the halter. It was nothing but a ragged remnant of a halter, truly not safe to use.

''Why did you ever put this one on her?'' she called.

"I was in a hurry," he said, his voice muffled by the wall. "It was all I could find."

"Were you hauling her to the vet?"

When he didn't answer, she turned to look at him. He was stepping down from the trailer, favoring the weaker leg as he reached the ground.

"No," he said. "I was stealing her."

Darcy stared at him. He appeared to be perfectly serious.

He walked toward her with a good halter, new, high-quality and embroidered along the side. It fit with the truck and the saddles but not with the looks of the place. She read it as he slipped off the old one and slid the new one on.

Rocking M Ranch, it said, and beneath that was the brand.

"Is the Rocking M mainly a horse-stealing outfit?" she said, trying for a lightly charming tone.

She smiled at him as she checked Tara's respiratory rate. It was twice what it should be, and the mare was sweating more than ever. Darcy flipped the mare's lip up to reveal pale, pasty gums. This horse was in trouble.

"Not usually."

He growled the words but he looked straight at her, his eyes and mouth holding that hint of humor again. His gaze lingered on hers for a long moment, too—almost as if he were seeing her for the first time.

"Tara's a special case," he said. "I don't make a habit of stealing just any horse."

"Why'd you pick her?"

He adjusted the halter and buckled it.

"We bred her on the Rocking M and sold her as a two-year-old. She won a lot in reining and she gave her all every time—she beat a lot of more talented horses. Her heart's as big as Texas."

He took the lead from her, and she thought he was going to walk away.

"What about the consequences of being a horse thief?" she said quickly.

He shrugged.

"He may come after me, but I doubt it."

"Who?"

"The worthless neighbor of mine who won her papers in a poker game. He neglected her. I warned him twice."

Tara's side rippled, and she turned to look at it. Again, she smelled the ground and thought about lying down.

"Well, God sent you to get her this morning," Darcy said. "She's in first stage labor. She would've died foaling over there."

"God has bigger things to do," Jackson snapped, his voice so bitter it chilled her.

Then, in a slightly nicer tone, he added, "Thanks for your help in getting her out of the ditch. I'll take her home now."

"You know," she said, "I should just wrap that tail for you and scrub and dry the—"

"I've foaled out many a mare," he said.

Darcy's control snapped.

"Then how come you can't see that she's sick, as well as in labor? That she's sweating like mad and acting as if she's going down? Her mucous membranes are as white as a sheet, she can barely breathe with those raspy lungs and she's dehydrated."

Jackson bristled and glared at Darcy.

Tara made her decision and lay down, half-on, half-off the road.

As soon as he felt the tug on the lead, he tried his best to keep her up, but she went down too fast.

Darcy wanted to scream with frustration, but then she was glad. Maybe this stubborn man would see that he needed help.

"Well, at least there's not a whole lot of traffic along here," she said sweetly. "In case you can't get her up, I mean."

Jackson threw her a furious frown, then he pulled and pushed, smooched and begged, but Tara ignored all that and looked at herself as if wondering what was going on inside her.

"If you're determined to let her foal here in the road," Darcy said, in a professional tone, "it'll be hard to have clean bedding for her if you can't leave her to go get some."

Jackson ignored that.

"Then there's the problem of keeping her from being run over, of course."

He gave her that frown again.

"Will you cut the sarcasm?" he said.

Something about the way he said it sounded as if they were old friends instead of strangers.

Darcy turned toward her truck. She might as well go. She had *better* go, for her own sake, now that she'd started hallucinating.

"Sometimes, this early in the process, they lie down just for short periods of time," she said, speaking over her shoulder. "She'll probably get up in a minute."

After a beat, she turned and added, "But then, you already know that because you've foaled out many a mare."

He glowered at her, then set his eyes on the mare. He dropped to his haunches, although his injured leg wouldn't bend well, then lifted Tara's head.

"I doubt she'd stay down long, anyhow, because even though it's early yet, this pavement isn't exactly cool."

She waited another moment.

"But then there's the fact that she's so sick she might just lie down and die."

"Will you just get over there, get your kit and get to work?" he snapped. "Instead of standing around all morning running your mouth?"

A great thrill of victory raced through Darcy's veins.

"Are you asking me to attend this mare as a veterinarian or as a woman?"

He looked at her, pushed his hat back so he could look at her with those fierce blue eyes of his. As his gaze moved over her body, she felt it as surely as the warm caress of a hand on her skin.

And she felt a curious desire to brush the hair that had fallen from beneath his hat onto his forehead. He had a farmer's tan—white skin where his hat had been that showed a clear line against his sun-darkened face.

After a long moment, he spoke.

"I reckon as both," he said dryly. "You've got no quit in you, just like Tara, and she's gonna need that more than anything. I'll supply the muscle power."

Chapter Two

Darcy turned and ran for her truck, her heart pounding because of Jackson's permission to treat the mare. She was thrilled to have won this battle, not only for the sake of the mare and foal, but also for the challenge of saving them. God willing, the struggle might take over her mind completely and let her forget about everything else.

Her heart was *not* beating so hard from the powerful way Jackson had looked at her. Yet she could still feel his gaze moving over her in that very *assessing* kind of look.

Well, if he'd been trying to judge whether she would respond to him as a man, she could tell him right now that she was not interested. Not in any man.

Despite that surprising, insane urge she'd felt—

*the desire to touch his face and brush his hair that
had come over her when his eyes met hers?*

Her little voice of truth wouldn't let her get by
with anything.

She punched in the handle of her equipment box
and twisted it, then threw up the lid. A horse's life,
no, two of them, depended on her right now, and she
needed to get her mind on her business.

Automatically, her hands flew to the necessary
compartments and began to make selections. First,
the IV catheter, needle holders, suture, cordless clip-
pers and a handful of Betadine solution packets,
gauze sponges and a bottle of alcohol. Then both her
hands were full. She'd have to come back for the
antibiotic injection and the bag of fluids.

No. Good heavens, she couldn't even think
straight! Everything would go much faster if they
brought the mare to the truck.

Tara's hooves scrabbled against the pavement.
Darcy heard Jackson kiss to her in encouragement,
and when she glanced over her shoulder, the mare
was regaining her feet.

"Bring her over here," Darcy called. "I want to
get a dose of antibiotic in her and start some fluids
before we walk her home."

He frowned.

"You're the one saying she'll foal any minute,"
he said, leading Tara toward her. "Can't it wait until
we get her to the barn?"

That annoyed Darcy thoroughly, although it was a natural enough question.

"I thought you hired me to make these decisions," she said. Then, less sharply, she added, "Hold her right here, please, with her head as still as possible."

Jackson did as she asked.

"This won't take a minute," Darcy said, quickly clipping a small patch of hair over the mare's jugular vein.

She scrubbed the site with Betadine, judged the best spot and, in a fluid motion, jabbed the IV catheter into the vein. She began to sew it in place. Tara's hooves moved restlessly in the gravel at the side of the road but, like most horses, she didn't seem too bothered by the procedure. Jackson murmured to her in his low, rich voice and stroked her with his gloved hand.

"You'll probably need to take off your gloves to carry the fluid bag," Darcy said, "so it won't slip. You'll have to hold it above your head to get it to flow through the tubing."

Jackson stood silent.

When she could look up, she glanced at him.

"You'll have to carry it," she said. "I'm too short to hold it high enough for gravity to work."

He stared, almost glaring at her.

"I'll carry it," he snapped.

"Well, then," she snapped back at him, "we don't have to worry, do we?"

What an ill-tempered man! This could shape up to

be the most nerve-racking foal watch of her entire career.

She should've kept on going south. She shouldn't have stopped—she'd known that when she did it. This was just one more time when she should've followed her instincts.

But she had stopped, and this mare might've died if she hadn't, so the thing to do was make the best of the situation and ignore the mercurial Jackson Whoever as much as possible. She'd simply do her Good Samaritan deed, deliver the foal and be on her way.

This mare is going to need IV antibiotics and fluids for days.

There it was again, her eternal, tormenting little voice of truth. Well, it was right. But that didn't matter; as soon as this foal was on the ground, Jackson could call another veterinarian. A male veterinarian.

She ran a short IV line to the mare's mane and tied it off. Then she drew up the antibiotic injection and pushed it in the catheter.

"Hold her here a second longer. I'll get the antibiotic into her, then we'll head for the barn."

He didn't say a word.

They stood in silence while she finished the injection.

"All right, that's good," she said, as she started putting things away. "We're ready for the fluids now."

Jackson didn't reply, which roused her temper all over again.

"I didn't mean to offend you by asking you to do something," she said tartly, as she dropped her instruments into the container and picked up the bag. "But gravity is the key. Therefore, the bag has to be above the horse's neck, and I'm not tall enough to hold it there."

No answer to that, either.

Quickly, she placed the IV line into the port of the bag of fluids and ran the liquid out until all the air bubbles were gone.

She turned to the mare, holding the bag in one hand. Jackson stepped forward and took it from her, held it above Tara's neck.

"Let's go," he said harshly.

Fury raced through her. Ungrateful wretch.

But she bit her tongue and did what she had to do, forcing her thoughts to focus on the mare, only the mare.

"Done," she said.

Jackson kept the bag high with one hand and held the lead rope with the other as he began to walk away. Stubbornly, he still wore both gloves.

Darcy closed the lid of her box and turned to follow. Somehow, he seemed to know that without even looking at her.

"I'll take Tara," he said, throwing the words over his shoulder. "You bring the truck."

Resentment flared in her blood. She opened her

mouth to refuse—and not only to spite him, either. Her instinct was to stay with Tara the whole way and return for the truck once the mare was settled in a clean foaling stall.

He was right, though. She might need her instruments and medicines in a hurry, and he couldn't run back for the truck if she needed to stay with the mare.

Maybe he was thinking the very same thing but didn't want to say it. He'd proved sensitive to his physical limitations when she'd stopped on the road.

Or maybe he was such a take-charge kind of guy that he needed to control every move she made now that he'd given in to her request to treat the mare. She didn't care. All she cared about was this good mare and her baby.

She ran to her truck, jerked open the door and jumped into the driver's seat. For an instant, she sat there and watched him and Tara, veering off the road to head across the pasture.

People became emotional and crotchety and short-tempered and unreasonable when their favorite animals were sick. Jackson admired Tara and liked her, and apparently she was worth quite a bit as a broodmare. Plus he'd had to steal her to get help for her. All that, with a tire blowout to boot, was enough to make him hard to deal with—that plus his prejudice about women equine veterinarians.

Jackson led the mare across the pasture toward the gate at a good, fast clip. At least, for him it was, now that lameness slowed his every step. He heard the motor start on Dr. Darcy Hart's truck.

Thank goodness she couldn't drive along beside him the whole way—she'd have to go around by the ranch road while he cut across the field. At least he'd have a few minutes of peace before they all reached the barn.

His blood chilled at the thought. What had he done, letting this pushy, interfering woman come onto his place, his refuge?

Just imagining her in his barn, perhaps even in his house—and no telling for how long—made him feel sick. It brought back the lurking nausea that had been his constant companion in those first horrid weeks of consciousness after the wreck. In a year and three months, the only person he'd allowed anywhere near his house and barn, his little corner of the Rocking M Ranch, was his mother.

And he'd never been gone very long from it himself. He'd learned it didn't take long to become a hermit who had no use for other people.

"Don't let that bag slip out of your grip," Darcy Hart called as she drove slowly down the ranch road while he crossed the ditch. "Hold it above her neck and keep her moving."

Know-it-all woman horse doctor.

His tongue itched to tell her to turn around, go out to the state road and keep driving, to get out of his sight and never come back. But Tara's life was at stake.

"Fresh straw's in the aisle," he called. "Turn in at the barn nearest the house."

Much as he needed the relief of being rid of her, he would force his raw nerves to cope. This mare was not going to die—she'd already been through far too much, and he was going to save her if it hare-lipped the governor. And the foal, too.

Dr. Darcy Hart moved on down the road, but slowly, as if hovering and watching every limping step he took would do some good somehow. The woman was a control freak.

But who cared? He didn't. All that mattered to him was that she prove to be as skillful as she was stub-born.

That and getting Tara to a stall before she went down to foal.

He set his jaw and made his aching leg move faster.

By the time he reached the barn, the bright red truck was backed up at right angles to the door. He led Tara in and down the aisle, ignoring the discomfort that flooded him. Darcy had already invaded his private space. Another person, a stranger, was here with him, and he didn't like that.

"I'm thinking this stall. Any objections?"

Darcy's voice came from the center stall on the right, marked by its door swinging open. He stopped and looked in.

"No," he said. "That's fine. It's the biggest."

She was stretching up, standing on the folding ladder from the feed room, threading a piece of baling wire around a rafter. As he watched, she twisted the two ends of it together into a hook.

"It took me a minute to realize the stalls weren't all the same size," she said. "This barn is really old, isn't it?"

He certainly wasn't going to be drawn into a lot of idle palavering.

"Right," he said brusquely.

"Hang the bag on this," she said, just as brusquely, "and then we need some more straw. I just spread one bale in a hurry, for fear she'd be trying to go down as soon as you got her in here."

He felt a vague irritation that he had read her wrong. Evidently, she didn't want any idle palavering, either.

"I'll get some more," he said, "I like it deep."

He'd show her that he did, indeed, know how to foal out a mare. He led Tara into the stall, tied her, hung the fluids bag and went for more bedding.

"I think her water's about to break," Darcy called, running past him toward her truck. "I've got to wash her and wrap her tail."

He grabbed the first bale and reached for the wire cutters, then threw the straw into the stall with one hand. He tossed in another bale and another, following to spread them nearly before they landed. He clipped the wire on all of them as fast as he could with his clumsy fingers and started spreading the bedding with his feet, as always.

The game leg buckled beneath his full weight, and he had to grab the bars at the top of the stall wall to keep from falling. Instinctively, he glanced toward the door, wondering whether the woman doctor had seen.

Then anger surged through him—anger directed at himself. Why did he even care whether she saw and pitied him?

He set his jaw and took the manure fork from its hook on the wall. He never should've let her come onto his place.

He hurried into the stall and used the fork to spread the straw. Tara moved restlessly, tried to turn her head to look at him and kicked at the wall.

Jackson took a minute to pet and talk to her.

"This'll only take a minute—I should've done it out on the road," Darcy said, as she ran down the aisle.

She slowed at the door of the stall and came in more calmly, so as not to agitate Tara any further, then set her kit and an open canvas bag on the floor. A roll of vet wrap bulged in the back pocket of her jeans.

"But then, you may still be in the first stage, right, Miss Tara?"

She crooned to the mare, running her hand over Tara's hip and then gathering her tail to be wrapped. Jackson reached for it and held it while Darcy quickly tore open the package and wrapped the tail securely.

"You may only be wanting to go down and roll around and get right back up, but we're taking no chances, Missy," she said. "We're a careful bunch here on the Rocking M."

Jackson felt her glance at him. For a moment, he expected her to ask something about the ranch name or make some remark about it, but she surprised him again.

"Would you get me some water in that basin, please, Jackson?"

He took the basin and went to the pump.

We're a careful bunch, here on the Rocking M.

We. That was silly crooning to a horse, nothing more. The good doctor Darcy Hart didn't mean anything by it. She wasn't invading the place or implying any connection to the ranch, and it was stupid to feel that she was. He was losing his mind.

Having her—or anybody else—here was going to make him crazier than he already was, but the alternative was worse. He was going to save this mare if it was the last good thing he ever did.

He carried the basin to the stall, his awkward gait sloshing a little of the water out with each step. Doc was squatting down just inside the door getting something from her kit, and he splashed a little on her as he lurched into the stall.

Heat rushed into his face.

"Sorry," he muttered.

"No problem."

She stood and turned to him.

"Hold that for me, will you? This won't take long, and then we'll untie her."

He had to stand close to her with the basin of water, and then, with her between him and the mare, he had to look down at her—at least, at the top of her head. Her hair caught the sunlight streaming in through the window and shot flashes of red flame into the air.

Its color wasn't exactly red, though. It was more of an auburn and it was definitely, uncontrollably curly. The wind had whipped it in all directions, but she gave no indication that she knew or cared.

If that had been Rhonda, she would've gone to the house and fixed her hair, no matter how soon this mare might be foaling. For the first time in more than a year, the thought of Rhonda made him smile. She would never have become a veterinarian because the job might've caused her to break one of her perfectly painted fingernails.

Dr. Darcy's nails were short and plain, her hands small and sure.

Her scent was very different, too, almost like new grass or a fresh wind. Rhonda wore a perfume—

He stopped his feeble brain in its tracks.

If he needed any proof of his weakened mental state, that was it, right there. Comparing a woman who had been his fiancée with a woman he'd just met was nothing short of insane.

"Done," she said, throwing a towel onto her canvas bag. "Thanks."

"Glad to help," he said.

But for a moment, he couldn't quite force his feet to work, couldn't step away from her. Honestly, he wanted to reach out and touch her.

She glanced at him, her green eyes wide. For a long moment, her penetrating gaze searched his face while he stared into her eyes. The look held them immobile until Darcy finally moved back.

"We may have a little time," she said. "If this baby's sick, too, and even if it's not, this treatment's going to be terribly expensive. You may want to call your own veterinarian."

Well. That was clear enough. Had his feelings been so obvious?

He tried to conceal the embarrassment that suddenly struck him silent by turning toward the window of the stall. With an unnecessary amount of force, he threw out the water still left in the basin.

"I would've sworn you were begging for this job not half an hour ago."

She didn't answer.

He turned on his heel as best he could and took the pan to her, made himself look her in the eye. Just because a man was no longer attractive to women was no reason to duck his head to them.

"I was," she said calmly. "I'm just trying to give you an out if you want one."

That made him feel a little better. Maybe she had interpreted the look as regret that he'd asked her to stay. Maybe she hadn't recognized the attraction he'd felt, after all.

"The only vet around here that I'd trust with this mare is speaking at a conference in Albuquerque today. And I don't care what it costs."

"Very well, then," she said briskly, "it's you and me. Let's get this foal on the ground."

She untied the mare and unsnapped the lead rope.

Immediately, Tara went to the middle of the stall, circled and started to go down.

"Don't you need to unhook that fluid line?"

"No, it won't tangle," Darcy said, moving past him toward the mare with the same quiet efficiency she'd used before. "This coiled type doesn't."

Tara lay down, rolled from side to side, then struggled to her feet. She stood for only a short time, then went down again. This time, after two halfhearted tries, she lay there on her side.

Darcy went onto her knees to examine her.

"It's an almost undetectable stream," she said, "but her water has broken. She's in second stage labor now."

Tara groaned and tried to push.

"She heard what you said and she's acting the part."

Darcy looked at Tara.

"Let's hope her acting gets results."

A sharp fear stung him.

"You think she's too weak?"

"We may have to help her."

That wasn't a direct answer, but he didn't press for one. What did he want—assurance that the mare couldn't live through this because he'd waited too long to take her away from Blake Collier?

He set his jaw. Maybe he had made yet another of his famous mistakes in judgment, but this was one time he was going to win.

"What do you want me to do?"

Darcy glanced at him, then sat back on her heels and stared at Tara. Her face plainly showed that she was worried, yet there was a calmness about her that hadn't been there out on the road when she was insisting on treating the mare.

"Go get a bunch of towels," she said. "This baby may be sick, too, and we'll have to keep it warm. Blankets."

"Should I boil any water?" he said dryly. "Sterilize the scissors? Tear the sheets into strips?"

That made her look at him, and he realized, with a little shock, that that had been his intention all along. She smiled, and he felt positively triumphant.

"No," she said. "My stuff is in sterile surgical packets. But if there's anything else, I'll let you know."

Then she set her attention on the mare again, and Jackson felt lost. He turned and left the barn for the house, trying not to think about the deep green of Darcy's eyes.

It took him a few minutes to ransack the cabinets—he just threw his towels in the washer and used the same ones over and over without ever looking to see what supplies were in the house. His grandfather had been the last person to live there before him, and he'd probably done the same.

In a cupboard in the bathroom he found stacks of towels his mother must've brought over—recently or in Old Clint's time he had no idea. He grabbed one batch of them and two blankets from the old armoire in the bedroom, then hurried to the barn. Sometimes he'd give the ranch to be able to run across the yard again.

But at least he was alive, as his mother was fond of reminding him whenever she dropped by on one of her infrequent visits. Maybe someday he'd be glad of that.

He heard Tara's groans before he entered the barn, and they made him forget all about himself. The tortured sound was so dreadful that it hardened his will even more. Tara—and her baby—would live if he had to send the ranch plane to fly Dr. Ward Lincoln back from Albuquerque.

Even as he had the thought, he knew it was as foolish as a desperate child's. This would all be decided in the next thirty minutes, and this woman horse doctor was the only veterinarian of any kind, much less an equine one, in fifty miles.

And there she was, at her truck, getting something from her vet box.

"She's getting nowhere," she said, when she saw Jackson. "It's uterine inertia."

Jackson's heart thudded painfully.

"What can we do?"

"Add calcium supplements to the IV fluids. She's so weak we'll probably have to get hold of that foal."

She turned to the barn with her hands full of supplies.

"Let me put these things down and I'll help you," Jackson said.

"Not necessary," Darcy said. "Let's go."

By the time he'd piled the blankets and towels in the corner of the stall, she was standing still, watching Tara thoughtfully.

"Let's wait a little longer," she said. "Maybe she'll get a second wind and deliver on her own."

Thirty minutes later, after three more valiant tries on the mare's part accomplished nothing, Darcy spoke.

"She can't take much more of this, and neither can I."

She began pulling on a long, plastic sleeve. "Here," she said, tossing one to him. "Put it on just in case I need you."

For a second, his anger flared. He couldn't fit his glove inside the plastic sleeve, and he wasn't going to try.

"Don't do it all yourself," he said sarcastically.

"I'm not," she snapped, flashing him a surprised look. "You'll get your chance to be a hero."

"That's not what I meant, and you know it."

There was a trace of hurt in her voice. Guilt nagged at him. She had no way of knowing what his hands looked like or why he wouldn't take off his gloves.

Tara groaned again and strained terribly, but there was no visible sign that the baby moved.

"It's always better not to pull a foal," Darcy said. "But we don't want to let her get too weak."

She went down on her knees behind the mare and gently inserted her plastic-sheathed arm.

Jackson waited, watching her face, but it told him nothing.

"There's a front leg," she said, at last. "Now, where's the other one?"

Finally, after an eternity, she nodded, and Jackson let out a breath he hadn't realized he was holding.

"All right," she said, "there it is, and there's the nose—and, thank goodness, the sucking motion that says it's alive. Let me get that muzzle tucked in between those little legs and out you come, baby."

She worked for a bit, then pulled gently. Once. Twice.

"We're getting him out, Miss Tara," she said. "Come on, can you help me, girl?"

Tara groaned and tried again to respond, but she was clearly getting weaker.

Jackson awkwardly lowered himself to a half-sitting, half-kneeling position beside the veterinarian.

"Why don't you let me help?"

"Because you would keep on saying women

aren't strong enough for this job," she said, through clenched teeth.

She gave the foal another pull.

Sweat stood on her forehead.

"No, I won't," Jackson said. "Because you've nearly got him out, and I admit, right now, that you can do the rest. Let me help you."

"All right," she said.

She moved over, and he took hold of the small hoof that was visible through the blood and gelatin-like straw-colored fluid coming from the mare. He grasped it firmly.

"Ready?" he said.

"Just a second."

Darcy reached inside to position the other forefoot behind the first one.

"To reduce the shoulders in diameter," she said, "Tara will thank us."

She took a deep breath.

"Now. Gently, gently."

Together they pulled the baby out.

"Too little," Jackson said, as they broke the sac surrounding it so it could breathe. "Not big as a minute."

"Pretty head," Darcy muttered, and reached for her tools. "Let's clean out your nose, little one."

She used a turkey baster from her bag to clear the foal's nostrils.

"Towels," she said. "Let's get him dry and keep him warm."

Jackson reached for the towels and began rubbing the colt. Darcy stepped back as he started trying to get to his feet. He wobbled and wavered, but finally he made it to a tremulous four-legged stance.

"Little or not, he's got a lot of try," Jackson said.

She craned her neck to look at the baby all over.

"Little colt," she said. "How's he bred?"

"Some backyard stud that got in with her at the wrong time of year."

"That's for sure," Darcy said. "I heard on the truck radio the first cold front's due in here today or tomorrow."

She stripped off the plastic sleeve and reached for a towel.

"Lots of rubbing," she said. "Keep going. I'll help you."

He handed her a towel.

"My stars!" Darcy said. "Jackson, these are fine, expensive towels you've brought out here! And they're brand new, to boot!"

"Only ones I could find," he said.

She smiled at him while her small hands moved the thick fabric firmly over the wet colt.

"Spoken like a true bachelor," she said. "I'm guessing, but I'm sure."

He nodded.

"Be sure," he said.

Then he wondered why he'd said that. It didn't matter one whit between them whether he was married or not.

Was she?

Chapter Three

The baby's knees buckled, and he nearly fell. Jackson caught him and helped him to the straw where he lay weakly, not even holding up his head.

"Rest up a minute and try again, Stranger," he said. "You're gonna make it."

Jackson's deep voice vibrated with dogged determination. He pushed his hat back on his head and stared at the foal hard, as if impatient for it to get up again. He moved back to give it room.

Darcy's heart sank. To her, the tiny foal hardly looked strong enough to make another try. Yet Jackson clearly wanted that so badly that suddenly she did, too.

Not only because she naturally wanted the foal to live, but for Jackson's sake, to relieve the tension clearly growing in every muscle and bone in his body.

"He hasn't broken the cord yet, so let him lie there and get more blood from the placenta," she said quickly. "It'll help his circulation."

Jackson kept his eyes on the colt.

"Should you start an IV on him? Tara's in such bad shape, he's bound to need help of some kind."

The urgency in his voice pushed her pulse to an even faster pace. This was an emergency situation doubled, and her adrenaline was kicking in. Along with it came the calm that always carried her on its wave of total concentration.

Except this time it wasn't total. Jackson's reckless assumption that the baby would live was nagging at her. What if she couldn't save it?

"He looks okay right now, though," he said. "Except his size."

Dear goodness, the man was obsessing!

"He looks fine," she said calmly. "But I have to tell you, Jackson, with his mama so sick, there's a good chance he might have problems."

His mama was wheezing loud enough to be heard all through the barn. Even worse, Tara had lifted her head only enough to look over her shoulder at her foal, and she still was making no effort to rise.

"You'll have to be thinking about how aggressively we'll treat him if he does get sick," Darcy said. "In the meantime, keep rubbing him dry. I've got to see about Tara."

She felt Jackson's gaze on her as she began taking the mare's vitals and adjusting the IV.

"What do you mean, how aggressively we'll treat him?" he demanded. "We'll be totally aggressive and use every treatment that's necessary. Isn't that what you're here for?"

Darcy threw him a glance over her shoulder, then looked again. His jaw was clenched, and his eyes were filled with a fierceness she hadn't seen before. His hands never stopped moving on the foal.

This was more than the normal desire not to lose a newborn animal.

"You're a rancher, Jackson," she said, turning to the mare. "You deal with the realities of life and death every day. Most men in this situation would weigh the value of a no-name colt against the enormous expenditure of time and money and effort it'll take to save him if he turns out to be really sick."

"I don't give a rip *what* it takes," he snapped. "We're saving him."

"All right, then," she said soothingly.

For a moment the only sounds in the barn were Tara's harsh breathing and the softer echo of the baby's.

"If that's your attitude," he said coldly, "then why were you so dead set on staying to help these horses?"

Shocked, she whipped her head around to look at him.

The skin stretched tightly over his jawbone was white with fury.

"What do you mean, *if* that's my attitude?" she

cried. "I'm only facing reality, for heaven's sake! I'm not a miracle worker, you know!"

"What kind of a veterinarian are you if you don't care if your patients live or die?"

"I *care!*"

"Well, act like it. Let's get some colostrum into this baby."

An answering fury shook her to her toes.

Yet a terrible compassion was mixed with it.

Jackson's raw need for the foal to live and the quick, desperate look he flashed at Tara right then tore at Darcy's heartstrings. Did he love Tara that much? If so, why hadn't he bought her back long ago? According to what he'd said out on the road, he hadn't owned her for years.

At that instant, his need became hers, and she wanted nothing more than to save these two for him. Why did she feel such a driving urgency to keep sorrow at bay for this man? She didn't even know him. She had been forced to offer condolences to many a longtime client, but she hadn't felt this depth of regret.

"Let me finish with the mare," she said tightly. "And let that baby get some more blood, like I told you."

He didn't answer. Which was a good thing because she probably would've beaned him with her stethoscope if he'd given her another order right then.

She took her time, added more medications to

Tara's IV and knelt by her head to talk to and encourage the mare.

"Her color looks better," she said.

Silently, she berated herself for worrying about Jackson's feelings when he behaved in such an unreasonable, arrogant manner toward her. Yet she went on trying to reassure him.

"Maybe her body'll start fighting the infection now that the birth is over and we're getting some medication in her," she said.

"Maybe we should bring in a wet nurse for the foal after he gets the colostrum," he said. "Take some stress off her."

"We'll see," she said.

Darcy gave Tara another loving caress, then got up and stepped around her to go to the foal.

"He's lifted his head again a couple of times," Jackson said.

As he spoke, the colt started struggling to rise again, and Jackson moved back to give him room. Darcy stayed where she was.

"You can do it, Stranger," Jackson murmured.

The satisfaction flowing in his voice touched Darcy again.

Oh, Lord, help me save this baby.

The foal staggered to his feet and took a step.

"Good," Darcy said. "He broke the cord that time. Let me look that over and swab on the disinfectant, then we'll see about letting him nurse."

Stranger's knees started to collapse. He went down

in a sudden heap. Tara stirred, looked at him, then lifted her head and tried to get her hind feet under her.

Clearly, there was no way she had the strength to accomplish her purpose.

"She may try again in a minute," Darcy said, as she looked in her bag for the Novalsan. "And she might step on him. Let's move him to her head and they can get acquainted."

Jackson stood up. It was an awkward task for him to bend and pick up the foal with his stiff, lame leg, but Darcy resisted trying to help, and he managed fine.

Carefully, he placed the baby under Tara's nose.

"Just keep on drying and warming him," Darcy said, as he scooted over to make room for her to kneel and care for the colt.

"No urine leakage, no hemorrhage, no swelling," she murmured, and then wondered again at herself while she swabbed on the disinfectant.

Here she was, sharing every scrap of encouraging information, which, in the long run, might turn out to be only feeding false hope to this man. She'd better keep her own counsel, as was her habit.

Sure enough, Jackson gave a sigh of relief.

"He'll be able to stand and nurse in a few minutes," he said. "I'm sure of it."

Darcy's heart constricted, and she threw him a quick glance.

"Hey, now," she said, trying for a light tone, "who's the doctor here?"

His intense blue gaze caught hers and held it mercilessly.

"This foal's going to live," he said tightly, "and so is this mare. I set out to save them and I'm going to get it done."

The pressure of that expectation tore the lid off her quick temper.

"Why can't you see reason?" she cried. "They've got lots of sickness to fight and very few resources left to fight *with!* I can't guarantee they'll live!"

Jackson's eyes narrowed to slits.

"There's no guarantee to anything in life," he said harshly. "But I'm not going to see another good horse die from something I didn't do. Not as long as I can lift a hand."

The last words almost broke apart beneath the weight of regret in his voice.

It was a grief that filled the barn without warning, a misery that rose to the rafters. Tears sprang to Darcy's eyes.

Something terrible had happened to him, too.

Then, without warning, a realization swept through her like a searing wind. She had known that all along. She had sensed it. Of course. With his lame leg and his eternal gloves. Maybe he'd burned his hands in a barn fire that had killed a bunch of his horses. Whatever it was, it had washed him up as a wreck on the shore of the life he'd had before, just as her loss had done to her.

Her spine went limp, and she wanted to sink into the straw in a heap like Stranger. This was what her life had come to. She had let her terrible trouble take over her life completely. Not only did it fill her thoughts and torture her mind, but it determined where she stopped by the side of the road. This was why she'd insisted on staying to help Jackson.

Then another truth touched her with a beam of light.

Her own troubles had been gone from her mind ever since she'd started helping Jackson with his.

Tara snuffled loudly. Immediately, Darcy and Jackson turned to the horses. The mare had her head up and was beginning to check out her baby, nosing him all over, giving him a lick here and there. Stranger, too, had lifted his head, although he couldn't hold it up for long.

Tara stirred as if she might try to get up.

"Let's leave them alone for a little while, and maybe he'll nurse on his own," Darcy said quietly, and blinked away the tears she was surprised to find still standing on her lashes.

She got to her feet slowly, so as not to disturb the mother and baby. So did Jackson. He followed her out of the stall.

Darcy risked a glance at his fierce face. With his hat pushed back, she could see the sweat on his brow. It was also standing on his upper lip. The air in the barn was hot and close, and she felt physically and emotionally zapped, so he must be doubly drained with his long walk on top of all the stress with the horses.

Maybe acting as host would break him out of the trap of tragic thoughts that gripped him.

"I could use a glass of iced tea," she said. "Or a really cold Coke."

He glanced at his hands, then over his shoulder at Stranger and Tara.

"I'll keep an eye on them," he said, in an absent tone. "Why don't you go ahead."

Darcy kept walking beside him. If she left him out here alone he would only fall deeper into his sad funk.

"They'll be fine. We'll only be gone for a few minutes."

He was silent for a moment, then he seemed to bring himself back to the present with an effort.

"Tara's really weak," he said.

"She won't step on Stranger now that we've moved him."

Darcy kept going, and he stayed beside her.

But he said, "Help yourself to anything in the house."

"What should I bring you?"

"Anything. I don't care."

Just outside the door of the barn, he stopped, glancing toward some battered benches under the shed row as if he'd like to sit down. His shoulders slumped, and he stared into space.

Darcy stopped, too, and looked at him. The haunted expression on his face broke her heart. She couldn't, she just couldn't leave him out here alone with his ghosts.

"I'd feel like an intruder," she said, careful to keep her tone neutral and not plaintive, "in your home."

He threw her an exasperated glance, opened his mouth as if to speak, then snapped it shut. They started walking again, out into the sunlight and then across the yard.

"I need to call somebody about my trailer anyhow," he said, as if to prove he had his own reasons for escorting her into his house.

He made an impatient gesture with one hand.

"I'd go change that tire myself but I'm not going to leave Tara right now."

"It won't take five minutes for me to drive you to it if that's what you want," Darcy said.

He frowned and hesitated before he spoke.

"No."

They reached the house and went up the two low steps. Jackson held open the door into the screened-in back porch. Darcy walked ahead of him into a large, square kitchen.

"I've got lemonade, Coke, Dr. Pepper, bottled water…"

Darcy stood still, looking around in amazement.

An iron cookstove that burned wood filled a brick-lined corner of the room. A huge worktable was in its center. Old pie safes and cupboards stood in strategic spots. There were no counters, no built-in cabinets at all.

"This is like walking into a time warp!"

"No," Jackson said, throwing the words over his shoulder as he crossed the room, "there's a refrigerator and a microwave. And a toaster."

There were. And stacks of paper plates and cups on one end of the worktable.

"And I assume no dishwasher, either," Darcy said lightly.

He paused at the door of the kitchen, but not to respond to her teasing.

"Bathroom's that way," he said abruptly, gesturing to the right.

"Thanks. I'm just grateful that you have one."

He didn't pick up on that small effort to be humorous, either.

"I'll make a couple of calls while you wash up."

His tone said that was all the polite small talk he could take right now. He disappeared into the depths of the house. Darcy heard a door close.

She followed his path into a narrow hallway, turned right and found the bathroom. It was nearly as fascinating as the kitchen, with its single, columnar sink and huge, claw-footed tub that had also been rigged to serve as a shower.

As in the kitchen, everything was clean. Only a

razor with shaving supplies, a toothbrush on a shelf near the sink and a towel hanging crookedly on a rack testified to the fact that somebody lived there.

Maybe he was the outdoor kind who hated to be inside under a roof. He probably spent most of his time with his cattle and horses—she had vaguely noticed several nice-looking ones in a pasture and some in a pen nearer the barn.

Maybe his life contained only the bare necessities because he didn't care about anything more. Maybe he deliberately worked himself into a stupor outside all day and came inside only to collapse and sleep.

Exactly the same life as hers.

She realized that with a shock. Her house might seem homier than his because of the furnishings she'd chosen in happier days, but the way she lived in it was totally debilitating and controlled by hopeless regrets. She'd lived that way for a year and a half.

Only today, after all that time, had she discovered how refreshing it could be to forget about loss even for a short, short while.

That sudden thought made her feel disloyal. She wasn't forgetting about her darling son and her husband. Not at all. She could never forget them.

Quickly, to distract herself, she washed her hands again, very thoroughly, took a clean towel from a stack on a small table by the window and dried them. She hurried toward the kitchen.

A door down the hall remained closed. She assumed that was Jackson's bedroom. The open, arched doorway across from the kitchen gave her a glimpse of the living room.

She stopped and looked in. It had the same old-fashioned, unused feel as the kitchen. A large stone fireplace was centered on one wall, with several pieces of well-made leather furniture, their cushions shaped by age and much use, facing it. The longest sofa had a pillow propped against one arm and a quilt thrown across the back.

On the opposite wall, looking as incongruous as the big refrigerator did in the kitchen, an ancient oak table held some very expensive-looking stereo equipment. CDs, their plastic jewel cases catching the sunlight from the windows, were everywhere—in stacks on the table on the floor, on the seat of a chair.

It was the same as a wall of full bookcases in an acquaintance's house. Or the tack room of a stranger's barn. How could anyone resist such a true glimpse into someone else's personality?

Darcy walked in and picked up the case on top of the stack in the chair. Muddy Waters. She rifled through the stack quickly, struck by the wide range of choices and the fact that they mixed time and genres as did the furnishings in his house. Delbert McClinton, Jimmie Rodgers, Doug Sahm, David Ball, Howling Wolf, Jimmie Dale Gilmore, Bill Monroe. Jerry Garcia's short-lived band, Old and In The Way.

Lots of blues. Lots of high, lonesome sound.

"You find a cold drink?"

Darcy jumped and dropped an Emmylou Harris, which clattered onto the pile.

Jackson stood in the doorway, leaning on the jamb with one gloved hand. His blue eyes were intent on her, but he didn't look angry that he'd found her pawing through his things.

"Not yet," she said, holding his gaze. "I got distracted looking at your music."

He didn't answer. He just kept looking at her.

Something about his still regard made her say it.

"One time I heard an interview with Emmylou Harris and she said her husband asked her why she always chose sad songs to sing."

"What reason did she give?"

"I don't remember. I just remember thinking that it was true and that I hadn't noticed it before."

"Most songs are sad," he said. "Did you ever think about that?"

She shook her head.

A trace of a smile lifted the corners of his mouth. He really did have beautiful lips.

"It's a fact," he said.

"I'll think about it," she said.

Finally, he turned away.

"If there's something there you like, bring it along," he said, over his shoulder. "Might as well get Stranger started out right instead of letting him hear that pap on the radio."

That made her smile.

"Good idea," she said, as she hastily made three or four selections. "After all, we don't want him to lose his will to live."

She followed him into the kitchen.

He opened the door of the big side-by-side refrigerator and freezer.

"In a glass with ice or in the can?" he said.

"The can's fine," she said. "If glass means one of those paper cups."

"You can have glass in the house," he said, "but we're on our way to the barn. Look here and take your pick."

He left the refrigerator door open and went to one of the big old cupboards.

"I want to be ready," he said, "if he's not nursing by now."

"What do you want to drink?" she said.

"Dr. Pepper."

Darcy took out the soft drinks, then stood for a moment to marvel at the other contents of the refrigerator. It was packed with fresh fruits and vegetables and held two or three labeled casseroles and dishes that did not look commercially prepared.

"Did you cook all this in your microwave?"

He glanced up as he took a nippled bucket and some other things from the cupboard.

"Oh, sure," he said, in a lightly sarcastic tone. "Come on, let's get going."

She followed him out the back door, wondering what had shut the door on the past for him and changed his mood. The phone call? Her interest in his music? Whatever it was, she was grateful. They had a long night ahead.

She also wondered who really was the cook who filled the refrigerator.

At the barn, Jackson went straight to the benches in the shed row and looked in the window of the foaling stall. Then he moved away and gestured for Darcy to look.

Nobody had moved much. Stranger's head was up, Tara was still nudging and licking him.

Quietly, Jackson set the bucket on one bench and took a seat on the other.

"How long do we wait?" he said.

Darcy looked at her watch.

"They've only been alone about ten minutes," she said. "Give 'em ten or fifteen more."

She offered him his cold drink, and he took it. For the first time, she noticed that he was wearing clean gloves—just like the others, but not the pair he'd soiled when he'd helped to pull Stranger into the world.

Suddenly, she realized she should've opened the can, that he might have trouble with that, but he did it on the second try.

"One good thing is they're getting acquainted," he said, nodding toward the window as he popped the tab. "At least, now Stranger won't think I'm his mama."

"That's the reason I asked you to leave the stall

when I did,'' she said, teasing him. ''I knew after you picked him up that he'd be trying to bond to you and that could prove a problem at bedtime.''

''Insights such as that must be what makes you a famous horse doctor,'' he drawled.

But he shuffled his feet restlessly, then got up and looked through the stall window again.

Darcy sat on the other end of the bench.

''Jackson,'' she said directly, ''I'm going to do my very best to save your horses.''

He met her straight look with one of his own and took his seat again.

''I thank you, Darcy.''

He actually seemed to relax a bit as he leaned back and drank some of the cold soft drink.

''We'll have to pray as hard as we work,'' she said, ''but God willing, we'll have them on their feet and on the mend in a week or so.''

Jackson shook his head. He looked at the can in his gloved hands.

''I'll do the work. You'll have to say the prayers.''

Then suddenly, almost as if against his will, he blurted, ''Mine wouldn't rise above the treetops.''

The bleak acceptance in his tone chilled her.

''Why do you think that?'' she said.

''I *know* it,'' he said, in a tone of complete finality, as if he'd already said too much. ''I lost my faith months ago.''

Then he looked at her. ''How can you stay here

for a week? You were on your way somewhere, out there on the road,'' he said.

It was her turn to look away. She shook her head and stared across his back yard, watching the wind move the leaves on the trees.

"No, I wasn't."

"You drove all the way from Oklahoma going nowhere?"

"Yes."

He eyed her curiously.

"What about your practice?"

His voice was so gentle she wanted to lean back against the bench and just listen to him talk to her.

But he was waiting for her to answer, and the words rushed to her tongue because he truly was interested. In her. As a person, not as a veterinarian.

"My partner's handling everything. I had to get away for awhile."

He nodded, watching her patiently, waiting to learn more. About her real self.

It had been a long time since that had happened to her. Of course, since she never went anywhere but to work. And to church, but there everybody knew her story.

Yet, in spite of the fact that usually—almost always—she needed to share that tragic tale, somehow she didn't want to tell it to Jackson now. It seemed a shame to stir up her sorrow—and his, too, maybe— and ruin this pleasant moment that was like a gift.

"Can't even a veterinarian have a vacation?" she said lightly.

"Yes, but I'd think even a veterinarian would have a destination."

She could feel his eyes on her. He really wanted to know why she was here.

Yet when she turned to meet his gaze his eyes were gentle. He didn't mean to pry, they told her. He wouldn't want to make her uncomfortable.

This new, kind side of him lifted her heart. She grinned at him.

"You'd think so," she said, "but sometimes veterinarians are an unpredictable bunch."

"I'd have to disagree with you on that," he said. "Anybody can predict they'll always send a whopper of a bill."

She laughed.

"Typical tightfisted client," she said, "beg me to save your animals and then complain when you have to pay for it."

That made him laugh, too. He had a nice laugh, low and melodious. A laugh she would never have suspected when they'd met on the road.

"Don't worry," she said. "I'll adjust my fee for room and board. If you'll share the homemade food in your refrigerator."

He pretended to consider it.

"I'll think about that."

"Yes. There'll be a nice deduction for meals, so

long as they're home-cooked and I don't have to do any dishes."

"Done," he said.

"And you might get another small deduction for your luxurious towels. It's good that you'll let me use them in the barn, since I'll have to sleep out here. Be aware, though, that you'll need to make my bed with lots of straw."

"Aw, get tough," he said. "You sound like the princess in the story who could feel a pea under her mattress."

"I am a tender flower," she said, tilting her head to smile at him, surprised that she was flirting with him.

She hadn't even *wanted* to flirt with anyone since the accident.

"You need to be aware of that, Jackson."

That made him laugh again.

"I'm becoming aware of the fact that this so-called reduced rate of yours may not be worth the trouble," he said. "I've got a ranch to run, woman. I can't be at your beck and call all day."

She shrugged.

"Suit yourself. It's your choice to make."

He sighed.

"At last *I* get to make a decision."

"Just so you don't decide to run me off," she said, "because I'm already attached to little Mr. Stranger."

They finished their drinks and stood at the same time, without a word spoken, moved by the shared knowledge that they'd waited long enough. It was almost as if they could read each other's minds.

Chapter Four

When Jackson and Darcy entered the stall, little Stranger started trying to get up. He staggered to his feet and got there faster than Darcy thought he could. He stood wobbling at Tara's head as though waiting for her to rise, too.

Darcy went to take hold of the mare's halter.

"Maybe we can encourage her to get up long enough to let him nurse a little," she said.

"I'll try to tail her up," Jackson said. "This isn't her first colt, so maybe instinct will kick in and she'll really try to feed him."

But try as they would, nothing worked. Nothing could, because the mare was at the end of her rope. Tara struggled weakly, and that was all.

"Let's quit," Darcy said. "She needs her strength, and we're wasting it for nothing."

"Can you milk her out?"

Darcy sat on her haunches beside the mare.

"I think so. Where's the bucket?"

"Man, I hate to start this hand-feeding business," Jackson said, bringing it to her.

Then he stopped in mid-gesture, his hand on one side of the rim, hers on the other. For an instant, his torment showed plainly in his gaze.

"I'd hate worse, lots worse, to lose him, though," he said quickly, almost superstitiously. "Or Tara if she's too weak."

He looked straight into Darcy's eyes and waited. As if he needed forgiveness for complaining and she had to give it to him.

"I know," she said. "Every two hours rolls around in a hurry, especially at night."

He let her take the bucket.

"I don't know why I even said that," he said. "I don't sleep much, anyhow."

"Me, neither."

Jackson's steady gaze held hers, expecting, maybe, that she'd explain why she couldn't sleep. But, as before, it also said he'd understand if she didn't want to talk about it.

And, once again, they began to work together without needing words. Darcy quickly, carefully, began to milk the mare, but what she got was so weak and watery that she instantly knew it was no good.

She glanced at Jackson. He was looking between the colt and the mare with that fiercely determined expression of his. The confident hope in it broke her heart.

"Jackson," she said. "I think we're going to have to use a milk replacer. Do you have a cow who could give us some milk?"

He was out of the stall in a flash.

"It won't take me too long."

While he was gone, Darcy did what she could for both mama and baby. She remembered the look on Jackson's face and she worried.

What if she couldn't save them both? They could find a wet nurse of one kind or another for the baby, yet if he developed an infection, he'd still be challenged to live, small and weak as he was.

And Tara, too, might be another sad story. She was so run-down, so malnourished and then so sick on top of it all. Foaling had simply taken the very last of what few reserves she'd had.

Darcy prayed and tried to remember everything she'd ever learned about small foals and sick mamas until Jackson came back with the milk and they managed to get Stranger to take some of it from the feeding bucket. Finally, he had a cupful or so in his tummy and he lay down to rest again after that ordeal.

"I'm going to get another bag ready for Tara's IV," Darcy said. "I'll be right back."

She turned and hurried down the aisle toward her truck, squinting against the dust in the air, stirred by the rising wind from the north. Jackson had his hopes up again now that the foal had nursed a little from the bucket, and she just had to get away from him and get a grip on her own expectations. She was a professional, and she had to be realistic in dealing with him and the horses.

Lord, please give me wisdom. Make me calm inside so I can hear what You want me to do for Tara and for Stranger. Lay Your healing hand over mine.

The sudden sound of a powerful motor and wheels on gravel interrupted Darcy's prayer. She stepped into the much-cooler wind and a few scattered raindrops just as a large white SUV roared up and wheeled to a stop in front of the barn.

Rocking M Ranch, read the logo on the spare wheel cover, the flowing words with the M on a rocker as their brand painted artfully around a handsome horse's head, all done in gold with black edging. Darcy stared at it. Another fine, modern vehicle belonging to this house from the past?

The driver's door flew open and, just as fast, a small blond woman stepped out.

This might be the cook of all that food in Jackson's kitchen. He was a bachelor, he'd said, but that didn't mean he didn't have a serious girlfriend. Darcy's heart sank a little, and then she wondered why. After all, she wasn't involved with Jackson in any way except professionally.

"Hello!"

The lilting, youthful voice and the lithe way she moved belied the wrinkles at the corners of her eyes and mouth and all the living that showed in her eyes. Laser-bright blue eyes that saw everything, just like Jackson's. A much older sister, maybe?

She strode toward Darcy with her hand out-stretched.

"I'm Bobbie Ann McMahan," she said.

"Darcy Hart."

They openly, frankly, looked each other over while they shook hands.

"You're a veterinarian?"

"Yes."

"Was a horse hurt when the tire blew out?"

"No. Tara had a little colt this morning, and we're just trying to get them both on their feet."

"Tara!"

Bobbie Ann took only seconds to process that in-formation.

"*Tara!* I know Blake Collier didn't sell her to a McMahan. Dear goodness, what has Jackson done to himself now?"

Her blue eyes snapped just like Jackson's did when he'd ordered Darcy to get back in her truck and go on down the road.

"Where is my son?" she demanded.

"In the stall."

Bobbie Ann whirled on one booted heel and marched into the barn. Darcy grinned to herself as she opened her equipment box and gathered the things she needed. Jackson was a formidable man when riled, but in a real showdown she'd have to pick Bobbie Ann for the winner.

Because nothing and no one could ever be more relentless than a mother protecting her child—even from himself.

That thought pulled the ground out from beneath her.

She had failed to protect her son, who had been too little to make his own decisions. At least Bobbie Ann's was still alive, hurt though he was.

Her heart went out to the older woman. It must be terribly hard to be the mother of a grown man whom she truly couldn't protect no matter how hard she tried.

Darcy tried to banish the sad thoughts while she scraped her wind-whipped hair out of her eyes and fastened it loosely at the nape of her neck with a strip of rawhide lying in the tray of her box. She picked up the supplies and started to the stall. Stranger needed antibiotics and fluids, family fuss or no.

Bobbie Ann was standing over Jackson, who was kneeling at Tara's head.

"What were you thinking?" she cried.

Jackson's eyes flashed as he looked at her with his face like a thundercloud.

"I know what I'm doing, Ma," he said, his voice filled with resentment.

He turned to Tara and busily straightened her IV line.

Bobbie Ann refused to be ignored.

"Blake Collier's liable to be coming after this mare with a shotgun," she proclaimed, "and he knows exactly where she is."

"Let 'im come," Jackson growled.

"You'll have to look over your shoulder every minute, Jackson McMahan."

"Ma, get a grip."

He sounded nearly as angry as when Darcy had stopped to help him. Impatiently, he struggled to his feet, turned his back on his mother and went to help with Stranger.

Unobtrusively, Darcy glanced at Bobbie Ann, who propped her fists on her hips belligerently. But her blue eyes betrayed her. She was more scared than angry.

"Jackson, with you here alone all the time..."

Her voice trembled, and she stopped. Raindrops peppered the metal roof of the barn. Wind gusted down the aisle. No one said anything. Jackson wouldn't look at her.

Finally, he snapped, "Don't worry. You have plenty of other things to do."

Bobbie Ann refused to be dismissed.

"Well, I can forget about whatever those things are," she said, crossing her arms determinedly and leaning against the wall, "because I'll be over here riding herd on you."

He threw her a quick, surprised glance that made her chuckle.

"That's right," she said, "and you can forget about running me off. Your hermit days are over, son, since you turned horse thief."

Jackson barked out an unwilling laugh.

"Ma," he said, shaking his head in helpless exasperation.

"I guess I can wear some of Daddy Clint's old clothes," she said. "And I won't even have to go get some of mine."

That must have been so preposterous to imagine that it made him smile.

"Grandpa was a foot taller than you," Jackson said, "and sixty pounds heavier."

"I'll roll up the jeans and the sleeves. I don't dress up to shoot it out with Blake Collier."

Jackson laughed, really laughed, in spite of himself.

"Go home, Ma," he said, in a tone that was more a plea than an order. "Go home and torment Clint."

But then he looked into his mother's worried eyes and slowly gave her a heartfelt, indulgent grin.

"Darcy's here. She'll protect me. Isn't that right, Darcy? Didn't you say it'll take at least a week to get these two on their feet?"

Bobbie Ann stared, looked from one of them to the other and back again.

"Mom, have you met Darcy? This is Dr. Darcy Hart. Darcy, Bobbie Ann McMahan."

"Well, it took you long enough," she said tartly.

"You're losing your manners, Jackson, keeping to yourself so much."

Her intense blue gaze searched Jackson's face quickly, then Darcy's. She appeared to relax just a little.

"I'm glad you're here, Darcy," she said. Then she grinned and added, "Not only so you can watch out for this reckless horse thief here. You're much more congenial than grouchy old Ward Lincoln."

Jackson held onto his sudden good humor.

"I'm sorry, Mom," he said lightly, "but I'll have to tell Ward what you said."

"Go right ahead. I've already told him myself. Ward knows he's a grouch. What makes it worse is that he's proud of it."

Darcy smiled at Bobbie Ann.

"I know the type," she said, "so I don't even need to meet Dr. Lincoln. I can just imagine him."

She finished with Stranger and went to work changing the fluid bag on Tara's IV.

"Imagine Ward behaving all the time the same way Jackson does when he gets unexpected company," Bobbie Ann drawled, her bright eyes teasing her son. "Especially his mother, who only wants the best for him."

That set them back to square one.

Jackson scowled, grabbed the bucket Stranger had drunk from and started out of the stall.

"Gotta wash this before it dries," he said. "See you later, Ma."

"Manuel's coming to get your trailer off the road just as quick as he can," Bobbie Ann said. "That's what I came over here to tell you."

"You bet it is," Jackson said sarcastically.

Bobbie Ann watched him go down the aisle of the barn.

"That didn't fool him a bit, did it, Doc?" she said.

"What do you mean?"

"He knows I came over here to see with my own eyes that he was all right," Bobbie Ann said. "I try so hard not to hover, but Jackson in another wreck would just be more than I can bear."

"His injuries come from a wreck?"

Bobbie Ann hugged herself.

"Yes. It makes me shiver to think of it. A boy named Brent, Jackson's assistant trainer, died, along with three champion horses."

Darcy's heart filled with sympathy—for Bobbie Ann and for Jackson.

"It killed Jackson's spirit, too," Bobbie Ann went on. "That's the worst part for me, even though I hate to say it with Brent's mother out there somewhere grieving his death."

"How long ago was it?"

"Over a year now. Nearly a year and a half. It was an accident," Bobbie Ann said rhythmically, like a mantra she'd said a thousand times. "It wasn't Jackson's fault—he wasn't even driving. I cannot figure out why he's this devastated."

"He can't get past it," Darcy said, thinking of an accident *she* couldn't get past.

"No, and I don't know how to help him."

The wind, colder and sharper, whooshed down the aisle like a warning. But Darcy didn't know how to help herself, much less Jackson.

She glanced at Tara's IV line. She hadn't tangled it. Thank goodness Stranger was lying still in his bed by his mother's head, his little tummy full.

Finally, she looked up. Bobbie Ann was staring into space, her face full of sorrow.

"It isn't just you," Darcy blurted, in an awkward attempt at comfort. "At first he told me to get back in my truck and get on down the road." She bit her lip. That wasn't a very reassuring thing to say, after all.

"So you stopped to help him when the tire blew out?"

Bobbie Ann's sharp blue eyes were filling with frank curiosity.

Darcy smiled at her.

"Yes. He was unloading this mare as I was passing by, and I saw she had a lot of problems."

"I couldn't believe it when he said you'd be staying a week. I'm so glad."

"I am, too," Darcy said. "I'm already getting attached to these two pretty horses."

And to him.

She pushed that thought away. That most definitely was *not* her little voice of truth speaking to her.

Excitement and worry over these horses combined with lack of food must be affecting her mind.

Lack of food. That was another shocking thought. She hadn't felt hungry in a long, long time, but she definitely did now.

"Bobbie Ann, are you the one who filled Jackson's refrigerator?"

"Yes, I can't help but bring him food. He gets a little cross about it sometimes, but he eats most of what I bring. Otherwise, he'd never have good, hot food. Except for breakfast at Hugo's once in awhile."

"Is Hugo a friend of his or a restaurant?"

"A tiny café. Farther down the road you were on. Jackson hasn't been to visit a friend since the accident. They've all about given up on him."

Like her own friends.

The sorrow in Bobbie Ann's voice was pitiful. Darcy felt a terrible need to distract her—and, to be honest, to distract herself. All her bad memories would come flooding back if she dwelled on the sadness.

"Let's go out and check the weather," she said. "This rain's starting to make it feel a lot cooler, and you can help me decide if we need to blanket these horses."

With tears in her eyes, Bobbie Ann smiled at her—

a wise smile that said she knew exactly what Darcy was doing.

"Okay," she said, "but let me give Miss Tara a pat. I've always loved her, too."

She went to the mare and knelt beside her, stroking and petting her, murmuring encouragement.

"Sorry I've been ignoring you, old sweetie, and your little colt there. I was all caught up in worry about my own baby."

She brushed her hand lightly over the mare's nose.

"You pull yourself together so you can take care of this foal, hear me?"

Then, like a formal blessing, she laid her hand on the mare's deep chest.

"Get well, Tara, girl," she said. "You've always had heart. Use it now—for yourself."

Tara lifted her head and turned to look at her.

Bobbie Ann patted her neck, stood up and left the stall.

"I'm still trying to not worry, just to do what I can and let God do the rest for Jackson," she said, as they walked toward the big open door. "Yet I have lots of sleepless nights. Isn't that awful, after all these months?"

"You're only human, Bobbie Ann," Darcy said, slowing her steps while she thought about it. "We all are. That kind of faith is a long time coming."

"I'm thinking that's because it comes from a lot of living," Bobbie Ann said.

Darcy nodded.

"And a lot of praying," she said. "I don't have it yet, either."

Only this morning I didn't care whether I'd ever do enough living to get it, either.

Suddenly she realized she didn't feel the same way now.

They stopped in the open doorway and smiled at each other. Rain gusted in and pelted them with cold drops, but they didn't move.

"Feels sort of good after all the heat, doesn't it?" Bobbie Ann said.

She glanced at Darcy's truck.

"Has it been hot in Oklahoma?"

"For months. And dry. I'm so glad to see fall come."

This morning I hardly knew what season it was. And I didn't care.

"How long have you been a veterinarian, Dr. Hart?"

"Two years."

"Where in Oklahoma do you practice?"

"Owasso. Just north of Tulsa."

Darcy waited, but Jackson's mother didn't ask the question they both knew was on the tip of her tongue. She answered it anyway.

"I couldn't stand it any more," she blurted. "I got up one morning and suddenly I knew I couldn't keep on breathing if I couldn't see a different landscape."

Bobbie Ann nodded. She looked into the far distance.

"I've had times like that," she said.

They stood in companionable silence for a long moment, then Bobbie Ann said, "Well, I guess I should be going. Jackson doesn't like long visits, and I've already worn out my welcome."

A honking horn nearly drowned her last word. A truck and trailer, which Darcy judged to be Jackson's, were roaring down the road toward them. The rig swept to a stop in front of them just as Jackson came out the back door.

"Why, it's Clint!" Bobbie Ann said, clearly surprised. "I thought he'd send Manuel."

A tall, good-looking man got out of the truck.

"Hey, Ma," he said, with a conspiratorial grin for Bobbie Ann. "Good thing you're still here. I need a ride."

"This is my oldest son," Bobbie Ann said, as he strode to them. "Dr. Darcy Hart, Clint McMahan."

Jackson's brother had gray eyes instead of blue, but his hair, too, was black and he was a little bit taller.

"Pleased to meet you, Doctor," he said, and touched the brim of his hat.

Jackson came around the back of the trailer. Clint went to meet him.

"How's it going, man?" Clint said.

He smiled, but Jackson didn't.

For a minute Darcy thought he wouldn't talk to Clint, but finally he did.

"You changed the tire?"

"Yeah. Manuel's getting the bad one fixed. He'll bring it to you."

"I can tend to my own tires."

Clint shrugged.

"He was headed for town anyhow."

Jackson scowled.

Finally, Clint said tightly, "Did you or did you not call headquarters for somebody to get this rig off the road?"

He turned on his heel, strode to the SUV and opened the driver's door.

"Ma, if you're ready, I need to get back to work."

Bobbie Ann nodded calmly, but her eyes held so much sadness as she looked from one of her sons to the other that Darcy wanted to cry.

Then Bobbie Ann turned and looked at her.

"Good to meet you, Darcy," she said quietly. "I'll be seeing you again."

She went to the passenger side of the vehicle, giving Jackson an apparently casual wave on the way.

"See you, son," she said. "Take care."

Jackson did have the grace to look a bit chagrined. Stiffly, he stepped around until he could see Clint through the window.

"Thanks," he said.

"Any time," Clint said, with a dry irony.

Then he started the engine and roared into the turnaround to head toward the highway.

Jackson went to his truck.

"I'll get this trailer out of the weather," he said. "Cold as this rain is, we might get some hail."

Darcy watched him drive toward a long shed that sheltered three other trailers of various sizes and types. Jackson had been walking more stiffly just now. And while he'd been in the house that short time, he'd put on a jean jacket. The cold, damp weather was probably wreaking havoc with his broken bones.

It was his spirit that needed the most help, though, just as Bobbie Ann had said. He was wasting all that love and comfort his family was trying to give him. Somehow, if she had a family, she didn't think she'd do that, grief-obsessed though she was.

She turned and walked into the barn. Mare and foal seemed to be dozing. Tara's nose rested on Stranger's back. Darcy smiled. They needed this time alone.

They were snug, inside and in the deep straw, but if it got much cooler she'd find some blankets for them.

Restlessly, she turned and walked toward the door at the other end of the aisle. The cold wind and its sharp raindrops had stirred her blood and, even though she shivered a little, the barn seemed stifling.

A wheelbarrow full of manure sat beside the back door of the barn. They'd need to use it pretty soon, and the rain promised to get a lot harder. She could spare Jackson that much.

So she slid the back door open, picked up the handles and pushed the load out to empty it.

Jackson was maneuvering the trailer to park it in the open shed, pulling the truck forward, then backing again. He'd have to get it straight beside the other one on his left so as not to hit the pole on the right. It'd help for somebody to direct him—then he wouldn't have to get out and see for himself exactly where he was.

She set the wheelbarrow on the ground and ran across the barnyard and down the lane between the large turnout pens for his horses toward the trailer barn. The horses were all standing with their rumps to the north wind, ignoring the shelter of their loafing sheds. They, like her, were enjoying the new weather.

Jackson had his head turned to look in the rearview mirror, and he didn't see her until she tapped on the fender and motioned for him to bear to the right. The open surprise on his face made her laugh. He didn't smile, just gave her a strange look she couldn't read and looked in his mirror. On the next try, he slipped the trailer straight into its spot.

"Great," she called. "That's perfect."

She started to the trailer.

"You don't have to get out, Jackson. I'll crank it off."

He opened his door and stepped out as if he hadn't

heard her, picked up a piece of two-by-four sitting by the post and placed it beneath the leg the trailer rested on when not hooked up to a truck. He lifted the handle and let it drop.

Darcy bent over and reached for the crank, took it out of its holder and began to turn it. Jackson's gloved hand closed over hers. His grip felt incredibly strong.

His body, bent around hers spoon fashion, felt incredibly big and warm, even in the cold wind.

"You see to the horses," he said, in a voice that made it an order.

He pulled her hand into his as he straightened up, bringing her with him.

"I'll park my own trailer."

Her quick temper flared. What she'd done hadn't been patronizing at all. Any two friends hauling together—or not—anywhere, normally would work as partners to unhook a trailer.

Friends. What was she thinking? This man was a client and a grouchy one at that. The famous grouch, Ward Lincoln, had nothing on him.

"Park it, then," she snapped. "I only offered you a little common courtesy."

She walked away without a backward glance.

But she was ashamed of her impatience before she reached the wheelbarrow. He was in a lot of pain, and he'd had three visitors today when what he wanted was to be a hermit.

Well, too bad. For a week, at least, his hermit days were over.

She picked up the handles of the wheelbarrow, marched to the pile and dumped the load. Then she pushed the barrow back to the barn, set it in the door of the first stall she came to, got the manure fork from the hanger on the wall and began to pick.

She had to do *something*.

She quit for a minute and peeked in at her charges, then resumed work. Her stomach growled loudly. It was past time for lunch, and she intended to hold Jackson to that discount deal. Bobbie Ann was a competent, intelligent, complex woman and, therefore, probably a fabulous cook. As soon as she finished with this, Darcy would go to the house, whether Jackson was hungry or not.

When his voice came from right behind her, she started and nearly dropped the fork.

"I'll do my own grunt work, too."

His tone was so hateful it sparked her temper in an instant.

She whirled and strode to where he was standing in the doorway beside the empty wheelbarrow.

"Then you'll need this," she said, thrusting the manure fork into his hand where the handle made a little hollow thud against his glove. "I'm going to get something to eat."

As she turned away and headed for the house, the look in his eyes stayed with her. It held something else mixed with the resentment and anger. Maybe somewhere, deep inside, he had the grace to be ashamed of himself.

It hardly mattered. She was here to save these horses, not their owner.

Or their *thief*, to be perfectly accurate.

She sighed. Well, like his loneliness, that was Jackson's problem. The Good Lord knew that she had plenty of her own.

And He would forgive her for keeping her distance now.

Chapter Five

Jackson sneaked a look over his shoulder every time he threw a forkful of manure into the wheelbarrow. Darcy's truck was still there.

Why was he even thinking it wouldn't be? Before she would ever hightail it out to the highway, she'd nail him with a list of instructions about the horses and a bill.

Or maybe not. Him acting like such a hateful hard case might've made her so disgusted that she'd leave Tara and Stranger at his mercy without even looking back.

Fine. He didn't ask her to take care of them.

Well, yes, he did.

He was just a jerk, that was all there was to it, and she was a perfectly decent woman who had shown him nothing but kindness.

When he tossed the next forkful, he looked out the door again. The bright red Ford was still there.

For the moment.

He snapped his head around so as not to stare at her truck. This was pathetic. He shouldn't even care whether Darcy Hart stayed or left, meddlesome woman that she was. She was worse than Bobbie Ann, truth be told—always trying to help him when he didn't need or want it.

He opened a new bag of wood shavings and raked them approximately level in the stall he'd just cleaned. For tonight, he ought to see about blankets, too, or sheets, at least, with this sudden cold rain bearing down and the horses with no winter hair yet.

Resisting the urge to look outside again, he moved to the next stall. He *didn't* care what Darcy decided to do. He could call San Antonio and get a vet out here now that the urgency of the foaling was past.

Besides, from anywhere in the barn he would hear the motor start if she cranked it.

Quickly, he started on the last stall. Darcy's eyes were the greenest he'd ever seen, and the most changeable. They could be filled with sorrow over whatever huge troubles had sent her out wandering around the country alone, and the next minute they could be full of anger or teasing.

They'd certainly been flashing with anger when she slapped the fork into his hand and stalked away, and, to be honest, he couldn't blame her. She'd only offered a common courtesy about the trailer, and he'd reacted like an unreasonable sorehead.

If he was any kind of a man at all, he'd go in there and apologize to her.

As he went for another bag of shavings, he tried to imagine doing just that. What would he say? What would she say? Would she give him what-for, as he deserved? And *then* would she get up and leave? He closed his eyes against that imaginary scene.

Without a doubt, he must be losing his mind. He had a whole lot more to feel guilty about than a little bit of grouchiness. Besides, he had every right to resent being pitied.

I wouldn't waste my pity on you, mister. Although you deserve a truckload of it for being mean as a snake.

He grinned. When she'd said that, she'd meant every word that she laid on him, and he'd felt warm inside because of it.

Now, even though he was sweating from the work, he felt cold inside—all the way through to his miserable bones.

He threw the handle of the fork against the wall and hurried into the aisle, stopping only for a moment to check the sick horses. They'd be fine for a little while.

Ignoring his jean jacket hanging over the stall door, he headed straight for the house. He owed Darcy an apology. He'd hate for her to think badly of him, even if she did drive out of here in the next minute.

When he passed her bright red truck with Oklahoma Is Native America written on the tag, he slowed and scanned the inside of the cab. Looking for clues about her, he guessed. Looking to read her thoughts from the insulated coffee mug in the cup holder and the tooled leather bag in the floor and the square black case on the back seat and the Western straw hat hanging half off of it.

Could it possibly be that Dr. Darcy Hart, mysterious veterinarian from north of the Red River, saw him as a man and not a cripple?

Didn't he have enough good sense left to never get involved with a woman again?

Ignoring the rain soaking into his shirt, he crossed the yard as fast as he could and opened the back door. He might as well own up to it—he wanted the two of them to talk again, talk easy, the way they had when they sat on the bench in the shed row and drank their Cokes.

Own up to this, McMahan. You want to touch her, too.

Rain lashed the roof as he stepped into the screened-in porch, and the cold wind crannied in through the corners, bringing a reality that slapped him hard. He couldn't touch her without taking off his gloves, without letting her see his hands. One glance at those scars and distorted fingers, and she'd be gone, for sure.

The door slammed shut behind him. Too late to back out now. He went in through the kitchen door, forming an apology in his mind.

Darcy was running water on some dishes, evidently finished with her lunch. His heart pounded harder. Would she leave now?

She turned off the faucet and whirled around. Her hair had escaped its tie string to flame in all directions around her face, and her eyes held a high intensity that made them hot, too.

Jackson stopped.

"Stay," he blurted, "and I'll make you the best bunkhouse coffee you've ever tasted."

The look in her eyes softened. She knew an apology when she heard one.

She was still mad and a little hurt, that was plain in her face. But she was wanting to cross the room as much as he was, too.

She reached her wet hands behind her and took hold of the sink.

"Bunkhouse coffee?"

"The only thing I'm still good at."

The blunt words hovered on the heavy air between them.

"Not the *only* thing," she said, and gave him a wry smile that made his breath come hard.

"What, then?"

"Last time I looked, you were a pretty fair horse thief."

"My other claim to fame," he said.

He wanted to go to her, wanted it bad. He wanted to run his fingers, his *bare* fingers, through her hair. That scared him more than the thought that she might leave.

But she wouldn't—at least, not now. He could read her, too, if she only knew that.

He clamped his jaw shut and turned toward the stove. No way was he looking for this kind of trouble. All he meant to do was make a simple apology.

And keep her here. You meant to try to keep her here.

Maybe so, but he should've stayed in the barn and let her do what she would.

He went to the old cookstove looking for kindling, looking for the stove handle, looking for anything but the wide, green depths of her eyes. Their heat could set every inch of a man to burning.

They could forgive a man his sins.

"If you're making the coffee, I'll warm your lunch," she said. "I'll wait for you for dessert."

He let himself glance at her again. She gestured toward the square dining table and suddenly, for the first time since he'd stepped through the door, he could see, not just Darcy, but everything else, too. She had set out a carton of ice cream and the scoop for it. On one side, there was a glass of iced tea, a real plate, real silverware and the pan of peach cobbler Bobbie Ann had taken from the freezer to the refrigerator a few days ago. Darcy also had a book—

propped open with the salt and pepper shakers—beside her place.

Then, magically, he could hear everything, too. The sounds of Mozart drifted in from the living room.

Relief and fear rolled through him, the two feelings equally strong. Instead of leaving, she seemed to have made a nest.

He turned to his task, opened the stove door and took kindling from the box beside it. He could feel Darcy's steady gaze on him as he began to build the fire.

"From the name, I take it bunkhouse coffee can't be made in the microwave?"

She spoke with mock reverential seriousness.

He shook his head. No way could he trust his voice right now.

"We may be at cross purposes, then," she said, "because I just opened the windows to let in the cool air."

Startled, he realized that he hadn't even noticed the stiff breeze and the raindrops coming into the room. He had lost all powers of observation—he hadn't been able to see anything but Darcy the minute he'd thought she might leave.

Well, that'd be the last time for such foolishness. He'd get a handle on his feelings from now on—the relief he'd felt had been on account of the horses. Only them.

"No problem," he muttered.

He kept his face turned to his work, although he was dying to look at her. For no reason. Just to look at her.

"I ate some of the King Ranch Chicken," she said. "The other pans are labeled Seven-Layer Lasagna and Beef/Red Sauce Enchiladas. Which do you want?"

"The chicken's fine."

She went to the pie safe in the corner and took down some plates.

"Don't worry, I'll wash these," she said. "It's worth the trouble— I like to drink from real glass and eat from real plates."

"Aren't you fixing *my* lunch?"

"I'm making the decision for you."

That made him laugh in spite of himself. He reached for a match and lit the kindling inside the stove.

"Well, let that be the last one," he growled.

She sniffed as she crossed to the big refrigerator and opened the door.

"It's for your own good," she said, jolly as could be, as if they were better buds than ever. "Really, Jackson, all you have to do is trust me."

"You trust *me*," he said, answering in the same vein before he thought. "Drink enough of my bunkhouse coffee and you won't care *what* kind of plates you eat from."

He went outside for some firewood and to get a

handle on it all. When he came back, the microwave was buzzing, and Darcy was fixing him a salad.

"What kind of salad dressing?" she said.

"Ranch."

"Of course. What was I thinking?"

She puttered around while he got his fire going, and once again he had to fight the urge to do nothing but watch her. She seemed so remarkably at home in his kitchen, moving around in it with her sassy, swinging walk that should've belonged to a much taller woman, preparing his food with her quick, efficient movements that never hesitated, not once.

He went to the cupboard by the door to get the old, tin coffepot, then to the sink to wash it out and fill it. He set it on the stove.

"Don't you think it's strange for a chicken dish to be named for the King Ranch?" she said.

"What?" He turned and stared at her.

"You know," she said, grinning mischievously as she gestured toward the pan she was returning to the refrigerator. "This casserole's called King Ranch Chicken. Think about it. What are they famous for, there on the King Ranch? Santa Gertrudis *beef.*"

"And if my grandpa Clint had been on his toes, we could've been equally famous for Rocking M Ranch Bunkhouse Coffee," he said playfully, following her lead again.

He bit his lip and looked in to check on his fire.

"Which probably means it's coffee stiff enough to stand alone," she said lightly, as she went to the microwave oven for his food and brought it to the table. "If we start on it now we'll be totally wired by midnight. We'll probably never need sleep again."

"Guaranteed," he said, after a little silence.

He couldn't just let her chatter on, talking to herself, after he'd apologized—well, sort of—for being rude before. "No need to wake up for foal feedings—we'll already be wide-eyed and bushy-tailed."

"Yep. It'll be a long night, so you'd better sit down and eat up," she said, arranging his plate and salad bowl with a cloth napkin on a place mat he didn't remember having seen before.

He stared at it as he sat down. He touched it, then fingered the napkin.

"Did you bring this stuff with you?"

Darcy laughed.

"No, Jackson. I found it right here in your very own kitchen." She shook her head. "Your poor mother," she said woefully. "She goes to so much trouble for you, and you don't even know it."

Guilt stabbed at him, and he reached for his old resentment. Bobbie Ann *chose* to go to all that trouble. All he wanted was to be left alone.

An awkward silence fell. From the corner of his eye he saw Darcy biting her lip and looking at the table.

He felt bad for her. She hadn't meant to irritate him again.

He picked up his fork and prepared to make himself eat.

The music from the other room was the only sound in the house except for the crackling of the fire.

"You like classical?" he said stiffly.

"Sometimes when I'm upset, it's all I can listen to," she said.

More guilt sent his gaze straight to hers.

"I'm not fit for human company," he said. His throat closed, but he forced himself to continue. "I didn't mean to upset you."

Her wide green eyes held his. They told him that she knew it took a tremendous effort for him to say that.

"I understand," she said. "I do the same thing to my partner all the time."

She swallowed hard, the look in her eyes riveting his gaze. It held so much pain he wanted to look away but he couldn't.

"It's the helpless regret that drives us," she said. "Sometimes we just take the frustration out on other people."

Then she glanced at his plate.

"Eat," she said, "before your food gets cold."

He fumbled with his fork because of the glove, but he was used to that now and he managed neatly to get a bite to his mouth. To his surprise, the food tasted delicious, and its hot nourishment was a comfort to his whole body as he swallowed.

But he couldn't just sit there and eat. Never, ever,

would he pry into someone else's grief when he wanted no one poking around in his, but she had opened the subject up, hadn't she? Maybe she wanted to tell him.

I need to know what happened to you, Darcy Hart. I need to know.

He couldn't say that, of course he couldn't.

He took a bite of salad and ate it, too.

Then, softly, in a voice he hardly recognized, he said, "Darcy, what big regret do you have?"

She lifted her head instantly and met his gaze with a look that seemed to him grateful. Pride surged through him. He'd guessed right. He'd said the right thing to her.

"That I didn't protect my baby," she said, just as softly as he had spoken. "That he had the life crushed out of him while I was at a neighbor's pulling a calf. That I never told my husband not to ever, ever take Daniel with him on the tractor."

He made himself keep looking into her eyes, into those deep, green wells filled with sorrow, because for that one moment it was the only comfort he knew how to give. To look away would make her feel forever alone.

"The tractor turned over?"

For an instant she couldn't speak and then, when she did, she sounded as if she were strangling.

"Yes. The grade was a little too steep."

His ears still held the words, *my husband*. A strange hand clutched his stomach.

"And your husband?"

Sudden tears appeared in her eyes. She pressed her lips together helplessly, made a hopeless gesture with one hand as she nodded.

Finally she whispered, "He died, too."

He never knew he would do such a thing. He never intended to do it. But he did. He didn't even know how to comfort someone.

But he got up and walked with his clumsy gait around the table to her chair.

"Come here," he said, and pulled her into his arms.

She looked shocked, he remembered that from the glimpse he had of her face as she got to her feet, but he didn't even think about it. All he could do was fold her small body against his big one and hold it there. He knew no other way to help her.

A sharp fear stabbed him, the fear she'd push him away, but by then it was too late to go back.

The deep hollow of emptiness inside him, that endless, echoing cavern of loneliness that he lived with every day and every night made him do it. He could not see another human being in that same condition and not try to do something about it.

He could think of no other way to comfort her.

For the longest time they stood that way, with Darcy huddled against him as if seeking shelter from a storm, with his arms tight around her pressing her closer. Her hands were fists, poking his chest, her arms crossed over her breasts as if to hold her heart in her body.

He couldn't tell if she was crying or not. It didn't matter. He'd learned a long time ago that the same sorrow could be too deep for tears one day and the next too heavy to be borne without them.

He simply held her, instinctively, with the same force working in him that had sent him to get Tara early that morning.

Finally, Darcy relaxed and slipped her arms around his waist, laid her head on his chest and hugged him. He fumbled to stroke her hair, but the gloves only tangled in it, and he couldn't feel its silkiness. Its clean fragrance filled his nostrils, though, with a smell like oranges or lemons, though she'd just come from the barn. He breathed it in.

A frisson of desire, which he realized had been there all along—maybe—trembled through him. He let himself lay his cheek against the top of her head, just for one heartbeat, to feel her hair, to tell her he understood, then he stepped back and let her go.

He didn't want to start something here. No woman, especially not a woman like Darcy, could want him to hold her for any reason *except* for comfort.

She wiped at her eyes with her hand, and he reached around her to take the cloth napkin from beside her bowl of cobbler. He pressed it into her hand as she glanced at him with a trembly smile.

"Thanks, Jackson," she said. "I'm just going to

wash my face. You eat your lunch before it gets cold.''

He went to his place and sat down.

Her tone of voice had told him again that he'd done the right thing. He had helped her. He hadn't offended her. He hadn't known what else to do, and he'd had to do *something*.

Maybe he was fit for human companionship in one way, at least—he could understand the other hurting ones.

Restlessly, he took another bite of his food. It was still hot, it tasted wonderful, and it gave him more appetite than he'd had for a long, long time.

The fire crackled. The wind whistled a little and slapped the pantry curtain against the doorjamb. The water in the old tin coffee pot murmured—it might be starting to boil.

He would eat quickly and then it'd be time to add the coffee. Then they could have dessert together.

The sight of the ice cream, starting to melt around the top, and the two servings of cobbler Darcy had already dished up made him smile. The best way to distract her might be to try to keep her mind on dessert.

He froze with his fork midway to his mouth.

What was he doing? Taking on somebody else's happiness as his responsibility? With him in the shape he was in?

The tempting smell of the bite of King Ranch

Chicken on his fork drifted into his nostrils. He ate it. He ate another and some of his salad, too.

All he was doing was getting through the day, just the way he'd done for months now. Expecting nothing particularly good, accepting the condition he was in and the burden he had to carry.

This day just happened to have brought Darcy to help him—which, he now had to admit, *was* a good thing he hadn't expected—and he was trying to keep her here to save his horses. That was all.

But by two o'clock the next morning, he knew better. On his way out of the house with the thermos refilled from yet another pot of bunkhouse coffee, Jackson stumbled off the bottom step and onto the truth.

He was hurrying recklessly through the dark to get back to Darcy.

Darcy was already with the horses. He wasn't wanting her here just for them.

He continued to walk faster than his lame leg could easily tolerate, watching the ground carefully in the path of light thrown by the security light. Actually, he was hurrying to Darcy because her presence was keeping the panther of panic at bay for him.

Horses in danger never failed to rouse it to full, snarling fury, and she was a good veterinarian who plainly had the healing touch. He was worried, but not alarmed, about Tara and Stranger. Darcy as a *veterinarian* was comforting him.

He hurried into the barn and down the aisle. That, and just the companionship, when he was so accustomed to doing everything alone, were the reasons he was glad she was here. After all, they'd worked as partners now for hours, turning Tara from one side to the other so her own weight wouldn't crush her lungs, taking care of cleaning her up from the birth, helping Stranger to nurse again from the bucket, watching the IV line, tempting Tara with feed and hay and all the rest.

No matter who might have been there to help him, he'd be eager to get back to the stalls and see if anything new was happening. He'd been alone ever since the wreck and had done everything alone. Therefore he had nothing to use for comparison.

But when he walked into the barn and found Darcy at the pump refilling Tara's water bucket, when he said her name and she turned to him with that million-dollar smile, a sweet, fierce desire ran through his blood. He didn't want to just touch her or hold her, he wanted to kiss her lush mouth.

He smiled back.

"Darcy Hart," he said. "Anybody ever tell you the name fits?"

She shook her head, the smile still clinging to her lips, her eyes teasing that he was babbling nonsense.

"What are you talking about, Jackson?"

"You. You've got the heart to work all day and all night and you can still smile like it's Christmas morning."

She threw her head back and stretched her shoulders.

"Smilin' at *you*, Mr. McMahan," she said.

His breath caught in his throat. The look in her eyes said that she meant it. The affection in her voice did, too.

"Only because I've done the cleaning up and the grunt work all night while you slept in the hay like a baby," he said.

She gave him a devilish grin.

"That's right," she said, "Jackson McMahan, veterinary assistant extraordinaire. I'll hire you onto my crew any time."

He laughed, too.

The warmth in her voice and in her green eyes just made him want to laugh.

"I know you better than that, Miss Sweet Tooth," he drawled. "You're smiling at this bag of cookies in my hand."

She raised one hand in protest, balancing the bail of the bucket with the other.

"No, no," she said, "I confess. It's really the famous bunkhouse coffee that makes me so happy to see you. One more mug of it and I'll not need sleep until I'm ninety."

"That's why my grandpa wouldn't let us kids drink it except when we mixed it half and half with milk."

She pulled the lever down to stop the water and started to take the bucket off the pump.

"Here," he said quickly, "take these."

He thrust the cookies and the thermos into her hands and lifted the bucket off, started carrying it to the stall. Awkwardly, of course, but somehow that didn't bother him so much now.

"What kind of cookies are these?" she said, from behind him.

"See? What did I tell you?" He threw a teasing glance over his shoulder. "You're only interested in the sweet stuff."

She chuckled.

"They're oatmeal raisin," he said. "My mom's favorites."

"*Danny's* favorites," she said, on a sudden exhalation as if she'd been hit in the stomach.

His heart hurt for her. Danny. She'd said her little boy's name had been Daniel.

He couldn't think what to say. What good could any words do?

"Jackson?" she said after a moment. "Did your grandpa build that little chapel? Or—it's too old for that, isn't it?"

"A couple of generations, at least," he said. "Mom could tell you exactly. The very first McMahan who settled here right after the Comanches were driven out claimed so many sections of land that he had to go to Mexico to get enough vaqueros. He brought back a whole village—women, children and old people. The chapel was for them."

"I saw the cross from a distance," she said quietly, almost to herself. "I'd like to go into the chapel."

Her voice sounded almost as if it would break.

"Any time," he said. "I'll take you there."

He was glad to see Tara holding her head up. He set the bucket of water under her nose and gave her a caress before he turned to Darcy.

Her eyes were filled with hurt. She stood still, looking at him but for a moment not really seeing him. Then she did.

"Remember when you said your prayers go only treetop high?"

He nodded.

"I feel God hears mine," she said, "but I don't deserve it."

Puzzled, he stared at her. "Why not?"

"I hate Todd—my husband—sometimes," she said, fiercely.

Tears sprang to her eyes.

"I hate him, Jackson, even if he is dead. I mourn him but I hate him, too, for taking the life of an innocent child and my life, too. Nothing will ever be the same for me. It was all his fault, every bit of it. He should've had more sense than to have such an accident."

His heart took a nosedive right through him and into the ground.

Then she would hate him, too. If she knew the truth about him, she would hate him, too.

Chapter Six

When the first fingers of dawn felt their way in beneath the sliding door at the south end of the aisle, Darcy was sitting on a bale of hay with her head in her hands. She had been feeling, more than seeing, the dark lessening, and now the proof of daylight lay across the dirt at her feet.

The night was gone, she hadn't slept any, and her eyes would attest to that all day long. They felt full of grains of sand.

Her *heart* felt full of grating sand. If she were an oyster, she could make a pearl.

But it was Jackson who should be the oyster, because he was in a shell closed tight against her. He'd snapped it shut all of a sudden, and she had no idea why.

Dear Lord! After a hug that truly had comforted her—*and* that was the last thing she'd have expected from him—and all that easy conversation they'd shared while taking care of the horses through the night, he had suddenly withdrawn and locked the door behind him. He hadn't said two words to her since.

And why, pray tell, did she care? This man meant nothing to her.

She sat up straight, arched her back to stretch it and got up to go see about her patients.

Jackson was gone to get more cow's milk. She needed to get out of here, too, even for a few minutes, preferably when he was here and ignoring her. He didn't even want to be near her.

So be it. She'd known he was a grouch when she'd insisted on helping him. She'd put up with it for the horses' sake, and saving them would be her reward. She didn't want to be with Jackson any more than he wanted to be with her.

But when she stepped into the stall where they'd spent the night with the sick mare and her baby, the memory of how his arms had gone around her so naturally came to her again. For one or two heart-beats, there, in his old-fashioned kitchen, she'd felt a bit of solace for the first time in a year.

And a twinge of desire.

Her mind skittered away from that fact. She would certainly never let *him* know that.

Probably it was because she hadn't gone into a man's arms for so long. For this whole, endless year.

But she did have to acknowledge that Jackson was an unusually attractive man.

Even old-fashioned grouches could be attractive.

Calmly, Darcy began to check the temperatures of the mare and baby and then she listened to their chests before she tried once more to get Tara onto her feet. The mare tried, tried again and did hold her head up after she quit trying, so Darcy felt better about her. Tara drank some water from the bucket, too, but only a little, since she was getting all the fluids she needed from the IV.

All the while she was working with the mare, though, and checking on Stranger, a storm of feelings built and built inside Darcy. She had to figure out how to live on somehow. It wasn't Jackson's behavior that was bothering her so—it was her own self, her own words. When she'd said to him that she hated Todd in spite of the fact that she mourned him, she'd finally blurted the truth out into the universe.

Of course, God had known that all the time, and she had admitted some anger toward Todd during some of the talks she'd had with her pastor, but she did hate him. And she did love him, too. She loved all the good memories, and they brought her comfort sometimes, but that hate never left her.

How in the world could any grown man be so stupid as to try to mow an incline with a child in his lap?

Dear Lord, please forgive me, but if Todd wasn't already dead, I would kill him myself.

She sat on her haunches and played with Stranger for a few minutes. He was all right, so far as she could tell.

But her own child was still uppermost in her mind.

She bit her lip as hot tears sprang into her burning eyes.

"I've got to get out of here for a minute," she whispered to Tara as she gave Stranger a final pat. "I'll be right back."

After throwing a quick glance around the stall to make sure everything was all right, she picked up her bag, turned and left them. The cross on the chapel had seemed like an omen about this time yesterday morning. She had felt a tiny hope for her life when she saw it.

Out in the aisle, she ran. She pushed a narrow opening in the south door, slipped through it and set her bag in her equipment box. Somehow, soon, she had to get some kind of control of herself.

She began to run again, through the cool morning that woke all her senses. All those hours in the barn had been more confining than she'd realized.

But no physical location was her real confinement. This hate in her heart and this eternal grief were strapping her down until she could pray only one prayer every day.

Strength. Please, dear Lord, give me strength to bear this sorrow.

Maybe if she prayed it beneath the cross that had beckoned her, she could find comfort.

Maybe—even if she couldn't pray for the sorrow to be taken away—she could confess the hateful feelings she held for Todd and pray for *them* to be taken away. Something in her rebelled at the thought, though. It was all Todd's fault. He and Danny would be alive today if Todd hadn't done what he did.

The path to the chapel was overgrown with grass and weeds, but near the door some small wildflowers bloomed. Or maybe they were left from a garden planted by whoever was the last McMahan to take care of the chapel.

But the cross brought her gaze to the sky. It gleamed white against the streaks of gray clouds fast blowing away to the south, and just as it had done before, it brought her heart to it, as well.

Not a comfort to her heart but her heart to it simply because it was there.

She ran toward it, her eyes on the cross, her ears listening for she didn't know what. She was on her way to the right place, and that was all she knew.

The heavy double doors creaked on their wrought-iron hinges as she undid the latch and pushed them apart. The sparse interior was dim, probably because the stained glass windows were dirty, but there was fresh air moving through and, with the doors open, plenty of light to see.

Several long, mesquite-wood benches remained on both sides of the center aisle, and the altar was there in front. Nothing else. No icons or artifacts. No podium. No musical instruments—no one would be careless enough to leave them when the chapel fell out of use.

Slowly, as she walked into the dim quiet, Darcy realized there had never been such instruments as a piano or organ there. Perhaps guitars or violins, back in the earliest days. Or maybe they had all been too poor for those, too.

She could almost see them, the earliest worshipers who had come to kneel in this place. They would have dressed in their Sunday best, probably scrubbed clean, plain cotton dresses and shirts and pants, some colorfully striped rebozos for the men, head coverings for the women.

Bright eyes for the children, some babes in arms, some toddlers like her Daniel had been.

Some of those mothers had been mourning their children gone to be angels, too. And wives their husbands.

In those days, on a ranch like this, vaqueros died beneath the hooves of horses and the horns of cattle. They—and their children—were maimed by ropes and wagon wrecks, and none of it surprised anyone. That was the way life was, always one step away from death.

And life had not changed in that way. Only now, people were surprised when it ended.

Old spirits, ancient tones sounded softly in the air. Darcy listened as she moved steadily toward the altar where she stopped and knelt in the dust. Stirred, some of it drifted into her nostrils. She sneezed.

Then she bowed her head onto her folded hands.

She meant to pray for the horses and for herself. She intended to ask God to help her deal with the hate she felt. She planned to share the load of her sorrow with Him.

But when she opened her mouth, other words came off her tongue.

Lord, go to Jackson and tell him he cannot live like this. Show him that he's killing himself. Please lift him out of his awful memories and let him see past that to the ones who love him.

Her own surprise stopped the prayer.

Finally she murmured, "Amen."

She kept kneeling there and listening to the words she had said floating in the air of the little church, listening to its mysterious voices, feeling its soul touch hers. Letting its solace soak through her senses.

What she saw against her closed eyelids was Jackson's face when he appeared in the kitchen doorway.

Stay, he had said. The word had come blurting off his tongue of its own volition, for she had seen the look in his eyes. He'd been as surprised as she had.

Somewhere, deep inside, Jackson didn't want to be alone, no matter what he told everyone.

She knelt there for a long time, the smells of dust and age and last night's rain drifting into her nostrils.

Jackson needs You, Lord. He has a lonely heart.

When she knew it was time to go back to the horses, she stood and turned, walked to the double doors, swinging open now. She paused, reluctant to pass through and to close them, unwilling to go out of this place.

But the horses needed her. She pulled the two battered slabs of wood together and hooked the latch. Then she looked around her at the blue sky with its streakings of clouds, at the ranch house so old it seemed to sink into the land, at the barns and corrals and pens with their horses lifting their heads to smell the wind, shaking their manes and tails into its billows, snorting and bucking with its power.

Darcy took a long, deep breath of the cold air, rain-clean and raw with freshness. She, too, wanted to run.

To stretch her legs and get her blood flowing— and to celebrate this tiny kernel of peace she felt inside. But how had it come to her? She still needed to talk with the Lord about her own self. And how long would it last?

Halfway to the barn, she glanced toward the two-lane road and saw a truck turn off onto the ranch road. A visitor. Well, that answered her question—if Jackson was back from milking that cow, peace was about to end.

And Jackson *was* back. She reached the barn before the truck did.

''Somebody's coming,'' she told him, hoping the warning would help him deal with the intrusion.

He had two bales of hay on the wheelbarrow and was pushing it down the aisle toward the back door. He gave her only the merest glance over his shoulder.

"My mom?"

Darcy followed him, going toward the stall that held Tara and Stranger.

"If sometimes she drives a black flatbed."

He stopped in his tracks, turned to face her.

"Look to be old? Rattletrap condition?"

"My eyes aren't that good. It was just coming off the two-lane."

"Could be Collier," he muttered.

His handsome face hardened even more.

The name made her stomach clench. Great. Both of them sleepless and wired with a long day ahead taking care of sick horses, and they had to deal with an animal abuser on the right side and Jackson on the wrong side of the law.

Mentally, she slapped herself to attention.

She was keeping her distance from Jackson and his trouble with the law and all his other troubles. She had enough of her own. Besides, the way he went from warm to cold in a heartbeat last night told her he was sorry he said, *Stay.*

It would be all right to pray for him, but for the sake of her self-protection that was all she should do. If Blake Collier was carrying a gun, as Bobbie Ann feared, all she, Darcy, could do was stay out of the way and try to stem whatever blood might be drawn.

Her heart started thumping hard. That black truck had been coming fast, with a purpose. Jackson wasn't armed.

She forced herself to speak lightly as she passed him and went to the stall.

"If it is Collier, where shall we make our stand?"

He jerked his head around and looked after her as if he'd forgotten she was there.

"Keep out of the way." He barked the words. "Go to the house. I'll take care of him."

Her patience vanished in a heartbeat. Her spirit may have just been praying for him, but her body had had no sleep at all and she didn't even *want* to try to cope with still another Jackson mood swing, this one turning him into an autocratic dictator.

"I'm going to stay right here in this barn," she said sharply, and shut the stall door behind her. "I've got patients to see to."

She did look at him, though, in spite of herself. He was dropping the wheelbarrow and heading for the open door.

A sickening dread gripped her spine. What if Blake Collier shot him, as Bobbie Ann feared?

The thought of Jackson wounded yet again, hurt even more, made adrenaline surge into her blood, made her mind race and her body tense to try to stop it. She took a step toward the door.

He had such a good heart, Jackson did. In spite of his hatefulness, he had a good heart or he wouldn't have stolen Tara in the first place. He had a good heart or he wouldn't buy CDs like those old railroad train blues songs of Jimmie Rodgers.

But he didn't want pity and he didn't want help.

This situation was man-to-man, and for that, he especially wouldn't want help from a woman. Besides, how would she help him if she went out there?

Resolutely, she turned and went to the horses. Jackson didn't need to be distracted right now, either. He needed to be alert. Yes, these horses needed her much more than he did.

Tara was acting stronger, but Stranger seemed a little weaker despite the fact Jackson had just fed him. She glanced into the bucket sitting in the aisleway. He hadn't taken all the milk.

Darcy looked him over carefully. He looked about the same, but he wasn't gaining strength, as she'd hoped. It hadn't even been an hour, maybe not more than half an hour that she'd been gone. Not only was he not better, she had a sneaking suspicion he was less so.

But why did she think that?

Maybe his eyes were a shade more dull. Maybe he didn't hold his head up quite as surely.

He appeared to be the same.

But he wasn't, and she knew it by some instinct that she couldn't cast into any scientific light known to man.

This sweet, tiny colt with the beautiful, baby-doll head was not coming along. She'd better get busy.

Automatically, she turned and started for the tack box in the aisleway where she'd been leaving her bag, but it wasn't there. Of course! She'd put it in her truck out of habit.

Outside, another truck rattled to a stop.

"Keep it running," Jackson said, his voice so hard and cold that it echoed off the metal walls of the barn. "Get off my property, Collier, and get off now."

Dread seized her. So. It *was* Collier.

"Give me my mare and I will," he said, in a voice that shook a little with anger. "You're nothin' but a lowdown horse thief, Jackson, even if your last name *is* McMahan."

He sounded totally implacable and full of fury to the bone.

Darcy hurried into the aisle and then ran down it toward her tools. Her only responsibility here was these horses. She would ignore the men and their argument.

Jackson wanted to fend for himself, anyway. He was a grown man and he could take care of himself.

Besides, she wasn't his mother. She wasn't anything to him but an emergency veterinarian, and he was nothing to her but an unwilling client.

"You've got forty-eight hours, McMahan," Collier said loudly, "and if that mare's not back in my barn, I'm filing charges against you with the sheriff. *And* I'm suing you, too. That's a Barpassers Image mare, and she's worth some money."

"Sue me for emotional distress, too, why don't you?" Jackson snapped. "Tell the world how torn up you've been without your favorite horse to starve and abuse."

Darcy ran out the door and to her truck. Collier was parked a little distance in front of it, and Jackson stood beside it, one hand on the fender to support himself.

At least there were no weapons in sight.

Collier's eyes went straight to Darcy. Rudely, he looked her up and down.

She gave him a hard look in return.

"So, McMahan," he said, leering at her, not even looking at Jackson as he spoke to him, "Got you a woman vet, I see. She any good?"

The suggestive tone and the look just flew all over her. Evidently they had the same effect on Jackson.

He started for Collier.

"I changed my mind," he said, "I'm gonna *drag* you out of there, Collier, and make you eat that insult to my friend."

My friend.

Darcy stared at Jackson while his words warmed a spot in her heart and her hands froze on the handle of the bag.

He was going to physically attack someone who'd impugned her honor.

No! He mustn't. Collier's bulk filled the window of his truck.

And Collier's hands had disappeared from his steering wheel.

Her feet were moving before she'd even formed a thought, and she caught up with Jackson only a little way from Collier's truck. He was fiercely intent, and she had to grab his arm to stop him.

He jerked free and whirled around, clearly furious. For one scary second, she thought he was going to hit her with one of his clenched, gloved hands.

She held up her bag.

"We've got to get back to the horses," she said. "This man's already done them enough harm."

In that instant she felt his focus change, although he gave no outward sign.

Then she looked at Collier.

"I'm good," she said, "but you have no need to know that since you don't give your animals medical care."

She returned his glare.

"Obviously you don't need a feed store, either."

Jackson's tension lessened.

"And right there's your answer, Blake, ol' boy," Jackson drawled. "I'll keep the mare and feed her while you visit with the animal rights people that'll be dropping by your place."

Collier gave him his full attention then.

"Better think it over," he snarled. "You'll wanna use that one phone call from jail to call your little wildcat mama to come get you out."

Jackson grinned at him. Actually gave him a thoroughly infuriating grin that made Darcy smile, too.

"Those PETA people'll probably bring along a bunch of TV reporters and satellite trucks," he said.

"You'd best get on home and make coffee for them, I'm thinking."

He turned and started to the barn as if Collier were already gone.

Collier's scowl deepened as he threw his truck into gear.

"Forty-eight hours, McMahan," he yelled hatefully. "Bring that mare back or I'm gonna own this place."

He spun his wheels and threw gravel in every direction as he gunned the engine and roared into the turnaround, but neither Jackson or Darcy looked back.

"What's wrong with the horses?" he said, and the urgent worry in his voice made her wish again that she could wave a magic wand and heal them.

"It's Stranger. I just have a feeling about him. Let me get his vitals now."

They hurried to the stall, and Darcy began a thorough examination. Stranger showed no change in his vital signs. She checked them again minutely before she dropped her thermometer and stethoscope into her bag.

"Maybe I'm imagining things," she said. "He's not coughing, and he did eat just now, right?"

"Right. But only a little bit. I was letting him rest for a while."

So they worked together and offered Stranger more milk. He took some more but not enough, really. They turned Tara and got her to munch some hay and drink some water.

Jackson washed out the bucket, took it to the house to soak in hot water and then came back, sat down and leaned against the wall to watch the horses for a bit. He was back to his tactic of staring at Tara and Stranger and willing them to be well.

"The cow's milk will suffice for a day or two," Darcy said. "But we could go ahead and get him the goat now and see if it'll stimulate his appetite."

"You think he's up to it? He's not too strong and that'd be the second way to learn to eat in two days, not to mention the third animal to learn to trust."

She frowned at him.

"Third?"

Counting on her fingers, she said, "Tara as his mom, you, me—seems as if the goat would be the fourth. Who are you not counting? You or me?"

He raised one black eyebrow.

"You, of course. Aren't I the one who always holds the bucket?"

She cocked an eyebrow right back at him.

"Aren't I the one who always helps him take it?"

The corners of his mouth turned up in the ghost of a smile. He had a very sensual mouth, she thought, and then realized that she'd thought that several times. Jackson McMahan had a beautiful mouth in addition to beautiful eyes.

"I don't think helping the foal counts."

"It had better. When we get the nanny I'll hold her and you can do the real work."

He gave a dry chuckle.

"Holding the goat may be more work than you know."

"No, no, you have to get a gentle one," she said, only pretending to speak sharply.

The silliness really felt good again. And Jackson had been ready to defend her honor with his fists, too. Both those things together made her smile.

"I talked to my friend who has a big herd of Nubians," he said. "I'd just need to tell him we want her now."

"Perfect." Darcy pulled the cell phone from her belt and handed it to Jackson. "Call him. Let's see if we can get a good nanny over here pretty quick."

She looked at his gloved hands and then shrank inside. Why hadn't she asked him the number and dialed it herself?

He realized the problem at the same moment and got to his feet.

"I don't know Terry's number," he said. "Back in a minute."

Darcy nodded, then leaned her head against the wall and closed her eyes. Silently, she said the same prayer for Jackson that she'd said in the chapel.

Then she gave thanks that the little church was there. That it had survived for a hundred years.

Jackson returned in what did seem only a minute.

"He's insisting on bringing the nanny to us so we can be here with the horses," he said.

Us. We.

"Great."

Awkwardly, with his stiff leg, he sat beside her again.

"Next time I see your mother I want to hear the whole story of the chapel," she said. "I love the way it feels."

Surprised, he glanced at her.

"You've been in it?"

"A little while ago. Do y'all not ever use it?"

"No. Ma goes to church in town. Caitlin had plans to clean it and fix it up for John, but then he got killed and we didn't think about it anymore."

"Who's Caitlin? And John?"

"John was my brother. Caitlin was his wife."

"Did she get killed, too?"

"No." His jaw tightened. "She caused the killing."

"*What?*"

He shrugged and turned to look at the horses as if he didn't want to talk about it.

"Refused to go with him on a mission trip to Mexico with some people from his church. Since he didn't have her there to protect, he took a chance and drove too far out into the boondocks. Bandits shot him."

Darcy clapped her hand over her heart.

"Oh! Your poor mom! And poor Caitlin! And you and Clint! I'm so sorry for y'all's loss."

His face hardened even more.

"We should've lost Caitlin, too, but Ma insists on asking her to Christmas and Thanksgiving this year," he said. "It's all Clint can do to deal with it."

"So Clint took it the hardest?"

He shrugged.

"Of us boys. Ma was wild with grief, and my sisters, too. Dad had been dead less than two years and it feels like we've lost half the family."

Dear Lord. Bless Bobbie Ann.

He must've done just that. Because before that, she'd had to go through all the horror of Jackson's wreck and now his hermit attitude.

"You have sisters, too?"

"Two. The babies of the family. They're spoiled rotten, both of them."

She saw his little trace of a grin when he said it, though.

Then he scowled.

"I have to run them off every week or so," he said. "Not only are they spoiled, they're a couple of little busybodies."

A sudden, silly prayer sprang up in her when she heard that.

Lord, please let them come by this week.

She'd love to hear what they had to say about and to Jackson and to watch them with him.

Then she prayed for herself.

Dear Lord, please give me back my sanity. I can't afford to lose it over this man and his family when I don't mean a thing to them.

Chapter Seven

Sitting there together for a long while, saying very little, they watched the horses. The thing that thrilled Jackson's heart was that Tara got up, all of her own will, and stood for quite a little while. Before she lay down again she drank from her water bucket and quietly munched a little bit of hay. Stranger, however, stayed in his bed, listless.

"Once he gets on the goat's milk he'll come right on out of it," he said, willing Darcy to agree. "He'll probably eat like crazy."

"I'm thinking so," she said.

She was suddenly quiet then, as if she'd meant to say more but she didn't. Jackson was glad. If it wasn't good, he didn't want to hear it.

The atmosphere between them was leavened with unspoken...not contentment, really, considering the sad facts he'd just shared about John, but companionship of some kind. He didn't want to spoil it.

"I'll put together some kind of a platform for the nanny goat to stand on," he said.

But he didn't move.

"What are your sisters' names?" she said.

He threw her a sideways glance. That was a fascinating thing about her. He never knew what she'd say next.

"LydaAnn—Lyda, not Lydia—and Delia. They're named for our grandmothers."

"Which one lived here?"

"Delia. Lyda was on the Reata, three ranches to the west."

"That's where Bobbie Ann grew up?"

"Right."

"I'm trying to imagine Bobbie Ann as a girl," Darcy said. "It's no trouble at all. There would've been tons of mischief in her eyes."

Jackson chuckled. "No question."

"Her eyes are the very same color as yours," she said.

A little thrill shot through him, and he threw her a quick look.

"I didn't know you ever noticed my blue eyes," he said, teasing her, inviting her to say more.

"Oh, no," she said, with big-eyed innocence, "of course not. I'm fairly sure no woman has ever told you what a marvelous color they are."

He laughed back at her, but he had a sudden, serious desire to grab her and kiss her. She was sitting entirely too close to him, and the whole idea was entirely too tempting.

There would be some real trouble if he started something like that.

Or, worse, if he tried and she pushed him away.

He got to his feet.

"Ol' Terry'll be along in a minute," he said. "He was already hooked up when I called."

Darcy nodded and crossed her arms behind her head, leaned against the wall.

"I'd get up and help you," she said, "but since that'd probably put another burr under your saddle, I'll guess I'll just grab a little nap."

He stared at her, surprised. Then he pretended to be shocked, truly amazed.

She laughed out loud.

"Get up from there," he growled. "Earn your keep."

But it pleased him. He wasn't accustomed to teasing about his touchy temper and ungrateful attitude. Well, at least not from anyone but his mother.

He tried to pierce her thoughts with his sharpest gaze. But she saw the glint of humor he couldn't hide.

They had to stop this playing with each other. It could lead to much more dangerous fun.

From the corner of his eye he saw her get up as he turned to go outside.

"Okay, okay, Jackson, I'll help. You don't have to get all grumpy and hurt my feelings."

He glanced over his shoulder, saw that she was pretending to pout. He flashed her a little grin.

"Oh, yeah, I forgot. You're a tender flower."

A brand-new warmth flowed through him. There'd never been a prettier woman on the Rocking M.

"I'm way too tender to wrangle a goat after a sleepless night," she said, following him down the aisle toward the stacked hay. "Let's hope Terry proves he's a real friend by bringing us a gentle one."

"Think about it," he said. "Goat wrangling may be exactly what we need to wake us up."

But I'm already awake. I don't want to miss a minute of the time you're here. The thought surprised him completely. He could hardly remember when he'd looked forward to anything or truly enjoyed the minutes and hours as they passed. He jerked his mind away from that realization. He'd better be thinking about feeding the foal.

He was a little awkward about getting his fingers underneath the wire, but he picked up the bale of hay and turned to her.

"Where shall we build our platform, Doc?"

The nickname made her smile. It always surprised him how much satisfaction he felt when he made her smile.

"How about right outside the stall door so Tara

can still see Stranger?'' she said. ''Inside might disturb her rest.''

So he put the bale down, end against the stall across the aisle from Tara's, and went back for another one. Darcy looked around for something to put across them for the goat to stand on.

Jackson watched her, read her mind.

''We can use that piece of plywood standing against the wall in the tack room,'' he said.

She turned and started to go get it to bring it to him.

''No, I'll get it,'' he called.

''I have to prove my strength,'' she called back. ''For the sake of my gender.''

His gallantry pleased her, though, he could tell. She liked him to do things for her but she liked to be independent, too.

He heaved an overly dramatic sigh.

''I reckon you'll throw that old remark of mine into my face forever. Why don't you forget what I said about women veterinarians?''

''Why don't you just go on outside and see to our nanny goat?'' she retorted.

Sure enough, there was the sound of wheels on gravel, and very close to the barn, at that. How could he not have noticed? All he'd been hearing was Darcy's husky voice. And, to be honest, that one word that he had used.

Forever.

Which was incredibly stupid for him to say. They

wouldn't know each other forever. She certainly didn't want to stay here forever. Well, surely she'd know that he most certainly had not meant a thing by it.

He *had* called her his friend, though, to Blake Collier. Maybe he was thinking they'd be friends forever—subconsciously, of course—because of saving these horses together.

They both stepped out of the barn to see Terry's dually truck hooked to his long stock trailer pulling into the turnaround. He opened the door and got out.

Immediately, he gave Darcy a big smile and touched the brim of his cap. He walked toward her, still smiling.

Jackson wished he could grab that cap and pull it down over Terry's twinkling brown eyes. Good ol' Terry always thought he was God's gift to the women.

They met at the back of the trailer where a big Nubian was tied inside by a rope wrapped in a figure eight around her horns. Terry glanced at Jackson.

"Hey, Jackson," he said, then turned his attention to Darcy again.

"You the people called for a nanny goat?" he said.

Startled, she stared at him.

"Well, aren't you Terry?" she said.

He chuckled.

"Yep," he said, looking her over appreciatively.

"Aren't you the beautiful woman veterinarian ol' Jackson mentioned on the phone?"

Her cheeks reddened slightly.

"I had no idea y'all's phone calls had been about evaluating my appearance instead of the nanny's performance," she said, a bit tartly.

Jackson stepped in and took over.

"I wasn't talking about your looks," he said. "This is Dunlap here just running his mouth."

He continued quickly before Terry could say any more.

"Darcy, I'd like you to meet my old friend, Terry Dunlap," he said. "Terry, this is Dr. Darcy Hart."

"And I can tell you right now that he *ought* to have been warning me about how beautiful you are, ma'am," Terry said. "I'd've cleaned up and shaved right quick."

Darcy laughed, then.

"No problem. We don't clean up at all around here. We just mostly live in the barn."

"That's all right. I've brought y'all a new roommate."

Then Terry leaned against the trailer as if they had nothing else to do all day but visit and gave Darcy his full, charming attention.

"You an equine veterinarian?"

"Horses are my specialty, but I treat everything."

He nodded, looking her in the eye as if to judge her sincerity on that. As if it were an extremely vital piece of information. Something about his attitude or his quizzical expression made her smile. That was Terry. He could always make the women smile.

Jackson bit his lip to keep from telling him to hurry it up.

"We veterinarians, equine or otherwise, don't have an easy way to make a living," Darcy said. "We're broke a lot. I take in all the antelope, possums, bears and llamas I can find."

Terry's brown eyes crinkled nearly shut, and he chuckled while he gave her an appreciative look up and down.

"I'll spread the word," he promised.

"Hey, Terry, ol' buddy, ol' chum."

Terry turned to look at him.

"Don't you think we need to get this goat unloaded and put her to work?" Jackson said.

They all looked in at the goat, who completely ignored them.

"All right. This here's Sally the milk machine," Terry said. "Where do you want her?"

"In the barn. I've got her a platform about ready, and that foal needs to eat."

He glanced from the goat to Terry.

"Not a good sign," he said. "You've got her trussed up pretty tight."

"Don't let that trouble you none," Terry said, unlatching the trailer door and swinging it wide. "Sally's a real sweetheart."

Darcy took hold of the door to keep it open, and Terry stepped into the trailer to untie Sally.

"She's good-looking," Jackson said.

"Only kind of females allowed on my place," Terry said, with a sidelong look at Darcy. "Good-looking ones."

Sally chose that moment of discussion of her good looks to prove that pretty is is *not* as pretty does.

She pushed forward and jumped off the trailer, dragging Terry with her in spite of all he could do. He hauled on the rope as hard as he could and went back on his heels in a futile attempt to dig them into the wood planks of the trailer floor, but still he slid along behind the goat at a fearsome pace and half-fell, half-jumped onto the ground, landing at a desperate run, propelled by a totally oblivious Sally.

The moment she made her first jump, Jackson tried to stop her. He ran forward, trying to catch her or head her off. But he didn't have a chance. Even someone with two good legs couldn't have come close to catching her.

"Whoa!" Terry yelled, his voice cracking as he stubbed his toe and went stumbling forward, keeping his feet under him by sheer luck and determination.

But the end of the rope flew through his hands.

Staring after her, Terry stood where Sally left him and ripped off his cap to slap it against his leg in disgust.

But Jackson wouldn't give up on chasing the rope. From the corner of his eye, he saw Darcy run across the turnaround toward the barn, and he thought they might try to drive Sally into the corner where the wall met the fence.

"Jackson!"

He glanced over his shoulder, saw that she had the same intention, so he widened the angle between him and Darcy to try to keep Sally boxed in.

"Here, now! Here, I'm coming," Terry yelled from somewhere behind him.

At that moment, Sally swerved, turned still more swiftly into a tight U-turn and headed straight for Jackson. He tried to step aside, but she was too fast for him. He staggered, threw out his arms for balance and almost managed to get both his feet solid on the ground. But then he went off balance again.

He gritted his teeth. When would he ever realize that he'd never again be as quick as he used to be?

Worse than that, he'd be humiliated when Darcy and Terry felt sorry for him and picked him up off the ground. That was his last coherent thought.

Sally reached him, shot between his spraddled legs with a perfect, unerring sense of accuracy, bringing her head up as she sailed underneath. The sharp blow butted him into the air with enough force to send him sailing. He flew a couple of yards with the whole world whirling and swirling in a blur of colors all around him and, after what seemed a year, landed on his backside, hard, on the ground.

On the drought-stricken dirt that had been too much like iron for even the rain to soak in. It knocked the breath out of him in one big whoosh.

He kept his eyes open the entire time, through sheer force of will and determination to have *some* control over the situation. The next thing he saw, after the wide, empty blue sky, was Darcy bending over him, her face pale and fear in her eyes.

But then, to his utter astonishment, she stood up and burst into laughter.

She actually, truly, stood over him and laughed.

"I...I'm sorry, Jackson," she said, gasping the words out between bursts of laughter. "I...I can't help it."

Terry joined her, and their two laughing faces hovered above him surrounded by sky.

"Your face is such a picture of shock," Darcy said. "Jackson, you're so funny."

Pure happiness flooded his whole being. She wasn't pitying him. She didn't pity him.

And neither did Terry.

"Get up from there, Jackson," he said. "We can't get nothin' done around here with you layin' down on the job."

He laughed louder at his own joke than he had at Jackson lying in the dirt.

Finally, Jackson got enough breath to speak, raised up on his elbows and looked from one of them to the other.

"Thanks a lot," he said sarcastically. "With friends like you two I don't need any enemies."

Terry wound down to a gasping giggle. Jackson saw that, miraculously, he was holding onto Sally's rope, which he must've managed to grab as she ran by him.

"What's the matter, Jackson?" Terry said, when he could talk again.

Sally started pulling him steadily away from the others, but he held onto the rope.

"Better practice up," he called back. "I've got you entered in the goat roping for Saturday night."

Jackson ignored that witticism and began the process of getting up. Darcy held out her hand to steady him before she even thought. He took it. For just an instant. No offense. No big deal.

A little flame of happy shock flared in him. She didn't try to give him any other assistance.

"How can you call yourself a doctor," Jackson grumbled, as he got his feet under him, "if you laugh at a man when he's down and helpless?"

"You're the one told me a little goat wrangling would be a good thing," she said, fighting not to start laughing all over again. "You awake now, Jackson?"

He cut a disgusted glance at her, but it wasn't real and he could tell she knew that. He dusted himself off with that same feeling of satisfaction he'd had when she gave him a hard time about being a grouch.

"Come on, Darcy," he said, raising his voice so Terry could hear. "Let's dunk Dunlap in the stock tank. He knew that little sweetheart of his would butt me halfway to Mexico."

"Nobody can know what a goat will do," Terry

yelled, holding up his free arm in self-defense. "Ain't that right, Doc?"

"That's right," she yelled back, as Jackson led the way toward his friend and she followed. "I'm sure you had the best of intentions, Terry."

"Hey, now, whose side are you on?" Jackson said, pretending to take offense.

He sent her a sideways glance that caught her gaze and held it. He grinned. He didn't know when he'd felt so good. He'd be sore tomorrow but he felt good right now.

"Think about it, Doc," he persisted. "Who's your client here?"

She returned the look.

"You are, but I haven't seen a penny yet."

Terry guffawed.

"And you likely won't see any, either, ma'am," he said. "I hate to be the one to tell you. He's tight as the bark on a tree."

Terry and Sally—neither of whom showed the slightest sign of remorse—had stopped dragging each other along and were standing still, watching the two of them closely. Jackson walked up to his friend and took the rope from his hand.

"Get out of here, Dunlap," he said. "And watch your back."

Terry grinned widely.

"Do your darnedest, McMahan," he said. "Whatever you do to me'll be worth it. That's the best laugh I've had since the time you tried to ride that black horse of Hank Scott's.''

He turned and winked at Darcy.

"You take care now, ma'am," he said. "I hate to leave you here alone with Jackson. He's a real side-winder when it comes to practical jokes. Try not to get him started, you hear?"

"*You're* the one got me started, Dunlap," Jackson growled. "Worry about yourself."

Terry was drifting toward his truck, but clearly enjoying keeping an eye on them as he went.

"I *am* worried," he said. "That's how come I'm not hangin' around to wait for breakfast."

Jackson snorted.

"This goat'll cook your breakfast before I will."

Walking backward, Terry grinned at Darcy.

"Anybody would've laughed at him, don't you think, Darcy? He can't cut off our groceries for being human."

Darcy chuckled. "That's right. And he has to feed Sally, too. She was only being a goat."

"There you go," Terry agreed.

"It's a starving foal we're trying to feed," Jackson called to him, and he started to lead Sally toward the barn.

To his surprise—and Darcy's, too, judging by the look on her face—the nanny went with him will-ingly.

"See? She's a sweetheart," Terry yelled.

Then he slammed his door, revved up his engine and went roaring off down the ranch road.

"*He's* the sidewinder," Jackson said, as they walked Sally down the aisle of the barn. "We've been tormenting each other since high school. I'll have to do some thinking now on my revenge."

Darcy only laughed. Jackson tried to look at the goat, at the condition of his barn, at the blue sky visible out the opposite door—anything but her as she walked down the barn aisle beside him. Her cheeks were still pink from running, not to mention from laughing so hard.

Remembering how she'd stood over him, laughing, he couldn't help but smile.

It probably wasn't really *her* that fascinated him, it must be the unusual color of her eyes. Or maybe he liked to look at the wild, curly mass of her hair that was also different from most women's.

Or maybe it was that smile of hers that, really, was even prettier than the sound of her laughter. When she did smile, he loved to watch the sadness in her eyes fade away, and it had certainly been long gone when Sally sent him flying.

He kept his eyes on Sally then, but he couldn't quite control the thoughts in his head.

Darcy didn't smile very often, but she had smiled at Terry as well as at him.

She had joked with Terry, too, as if they were buddies.

The little twinge of ill feeling he'd had when Terry

flirted with her tugged at him again. Terry always had been quite a hand with the ladies.

Which could be downright irritating sometimes. Like when he'd called Darcy Doc. He didn't know her, not a bit, and he had no business calling her by a nickname or trying to flirt with her, either.

The little twinge of feeling bloomed into a bitter flower.

It couldn't be jealousy, though. He had no reason to be jealous, since Darcy was nothing to him. Nothing but a friend.

She *was* a friend, though. To his amazement, he'd have to admit to that. New and strange as it was, they had a friendship forming, or she would never have told him what made her so sad.

And he wouldn't be glad she was still here instead of wishing she'd go away.

He took a long, deep breath.

Terry was his friend, too. And he'd for sure been all right when Jackson got dumped in the dirt—he didn't even ask if it hurt his leg and he didn't try to help him up.

He might have to tell Terry to take it easy with Darcy, though. Without betraying any confidences, he could explain that she had a lot on her mind and was not, like Terry, interested only in a good time.

"You want to put it together while I hold her?" Darcy asked.

Startled, he noticed they had reached the bales of hay, and he hurried to put together the little platform.

Sally jumped onto it like a trouper, and Darcy kept on holding her rope.

"Be sure and leave the door open so Tara can see Stranger when you bring him out."

Somehow, even the sound of her voice telling him what to do made him feel lighthearted.

"Yes, ma'am!"

He crossed the aisle and opened the door to Tara's stall.

"No need to be sarcastic," she said lightly. "Really, Jackson, if you'll just do everything I tell you—and without talking back—your life will be much easier."

Now that was the kind of remark that made him know they were friends.

He glanced over his shoulder and met her gaze for an instant. And then another. Even though he tried, he couldn't look away. Her green eyes were sparkling with mischief. Her full lips were smiling, and her mouth looked sweet as candy.

A little thrill—equal parts desire and fear—ran down his spine and into his veins.

Friends. That was all they were. He couldn't handle another rejection from a woman, not yet, anyway.

"Well, Doc, you're in a lively mood," he said. "Watching me get knocked on my ear must've made your day."

She laughed.

"I don't think it was quite your *ear* that you landed on, Jackson."

Her wide gaze never left his, and the desire in his blood began to grow stronger than the fear.

He scowled at her. "Don't be getting too cocky," he said. "You're the one closest to the butting machine."

"No, you're the milk machine, aren't you, Sally?" she said.

She turned to look at the goat and pet her, which was the only way he could get loose to tend to business.

"At least that's what Terry said," she crooned to the goat.

Jackson frowned as he went into the stall and bent over little Stranger.

Terry. Terry this and Terry that.

"Oh, Jackson, I only wish you could've seen the look on your face."

"It couldn't have been *that* funny," he growled.

But, as he began encouraging Stranger to get to his feet, he grinned.

Darcy hadn't made a federal case out of his dustup. She hadn't acted like his sisters and his mother. Terry hadn't gotten that pained, sympathetic expression like Clint's—or the masklike, embarrassed one—and come to help Jackson out of harm's way as if he were a helpless baby.

They'd both fooled him. They'd treated him just like anybody else, anybody who had been standing in front of a goat on two good legs.

Crooning to Stranger wordlessly, he reached under

the colt's belly with both hands and lifted him to his feet. He half-carried, half-walked him through the open stall door and into the aisle while Tara nickered and kept a close eye on them. Stranger called to her.

"It's all right," Jackson said, and somehow the words sort of sank into him and warmed him, "it's all right, little buddy. How about some breakfast if it'll hold still for you?"

Sally turned her head and sniffed at him. Stranger smelled her.

"She'll hold still," Darcy said. "Look. I think they like each other."

The pure happiness in her voice warmed Jackson some more. She felt the same way he did about saving this baby and, together, they would get it done.

He guided Stranger's hungry mouth, and Darcy held Sally.

"You're a good foster mother, aren't you?" she said. "Terry was right when he said you're a sweetheart."

Terry again.

Jackson set his jaw and concentrated on helping Stranger get into exactly the right position. With one taste of the nourishing milk, Stranger was nursing.

"See, Terry wasn't playing a trick on you, Jackson," Darcy said. "She really is a nurse goat."

"And Terry really is a trickster, whether this goat feeds this foal or not."

He bit his lip and felt ashamed. He certainly wasn't going to bad-mouth his old friend.

But Darcy didn't take it that way, anyhow.

"Some people just can't resist trying to stir things up," she said mildly. "And sometimes that's good for the rest of us."

"Right," he said, and watched her eyes turn an even darker green as she smiled at him.

Then she turned away, and they concentrated on the task at hand until Stranger's tummy was pooching out a little and he quit nursing. Darcy let Sally down off the platform so they could get to know each other a little better, then Jackson took the foal to his mother, who had been watching him all the time. Sally tried to follow.

"Let's put Sally where she can see Stranger," Darcy said. "In that next stall, okay?"

"Fine," Jackson said.

With an effort, he kept his voice level and his gaze on the horses.

But then he couldn't help it, he just had to watch Darcy with the nanny. She moved around the stall as efficiently as she had done in his kitchen, her trim hips swinging as she walked to the stack of bags of bedding, her small waist calling to his hands.

"Let me get her some hay," he said, and went out and down the aisle.

He had to get a grip on himself. He wasn't about to start anything—not with *any* woman—he had promised himself that for more than a year now.

Because what good would it do? How could any woman not feel the same way Rhonda had felt? What was it she'd said when she gave him back his ring? *You just don't seem like yourself any more, Jackson. You're a stranger to me now.*

Rhonda had never been known for her tact. He did have to give her credit, though, for using the word *seem* instead of *look*. Looks were everything to her. However, even for a woman with better values, he was no prize any more, and that was a fact.

He picked up a bale and carried it to the goat's stall, dropped it in the aisle and reached into his back pocket for the wire cutters. Good. He was glad he'd reminded himself of reality. That was his greatest pride these days—the fact that he was facing the hard, cold truth.

Darcy was kicking some of the shavings she'd dumped in the goat's stall to the side by the door. He opened it to take a couple of flakes in and nearly bumped into her. Awkwardly, he sidestepped and dropped the hay in the corner.

"Well, I'm with Terry," she said, and Jackson's pulse jumped into his throat.

He spun on his heel and walked to her.

"What about breakfast?" she said, raising her eyebrows at him as she shook the last of the shavings out of the bag and tossed it over the door into the aisle. "Or is that only for horses around here?"

She tilted her head and lifted her chin to look him in the eye.

"Are you determined to eat me out of house and home?" Jackson said, his voice rasping a little bit, low in his throat. "I've fed you all night long, gone to the house and carried snacks out here to you by the armload, and here you are, begging for more."

A sinking feeling pulled his heart toward the floor, but it was relief, not despair. She had only meant she was wanting breakfast when she'd said she was with Terry.

"Ha!" she said, and gave him such a look it nearly melted him. "Black coffee and cookies are all I've had since the one meal I ate yesterday. Room and board *are* part of my fee, you may recall. And I *have* been working nonstop for more than twenty-four hours."

She arched her back and stretched like a lazy cat.

His whole being stirred with desire. He couldn't take his eyes off the curves of her body, the natural grace of her outstretched arms, the shape of her slender throat, thrown into relief against the light from the window.

He wanted to hold her.

She cocked her head and closed her eyes, her lips slightly parted.

What he *really* wanted to do was kiss her.

But he turned away.

No way would he let himself even think about that.

Chapter Eight

Jackson got out of the stall as fast as he could and left the door for Darcy to close.

"What can I look forward to?" she said, coming along right behind him.

Not a kiss.

As if she'd even accept one from him, much less look forward to it. Like Rhonda, she'd probably be horrified by the prospect of his scarred, misshapen hands touching hers, never mind his mouth kissing hers.

He walked faster. Maybe he could get away without talking to her for awhile. They'd been talking way too much.

"Jackson?"

She was following him down the aisle.

"What d'you mean?"

He threw the words over his shoulder and didn't stop to wait for her.

"For *breakfast,* of course! What do you usually have for *breakfast,* Jackson?"

The lilt of humor in her voice lured him like a snatch of song. But he wasn't going to turn around and see that teasing glint in her green eyes because that would make him start thinking about kissing again.

He'd have to talk to her, though, before she hounded him half to death.

Still facing forward, he growled, "Whatever Ma brought that I can microwave."

There. That should be sufficiently grumpy to make her leave him alone.

But it wasn't.

"I was hoping for the bunkhouse coffee chef to cook me something personally," she persisted, still in that teasing tone. "Maybe something with biscuits. I don't know that a microwaved breakfast would satisfy me."

What he marveled at was that she was even satisfied to *talk* to him, much less tease and joke around to make this tension over the horses easier to bear. This was a beautiful, smart, high-energy woman here, and he had no idea why she seemed happy just being in his company.

But he had more to do than ponder that mystery, which, in the long run, did not matter in the least to his life.

He turned and scowled at her. Sure enough, she was right on his heels.

"You're as bad as LydaAnn," he said. "Pestering me for lack of anything better to do."

She caught up and walked along beside him, looking at him with an impish grin.

"I'm pestering you for lack of *food,* Jackson. What are you gonna do about it?"

He tried, but he couldn't resist grinning back.

"Show you to the kitchen."

"I cooked last time."

"Ha! You warmed something up and made me a salad."

She tossed her hair flirtatiously.

"Now *you* make *my* breakfast."

He shook his head. "Never know when to quit," he said dryly. "That's a dangerous trait."

"Or an admirable one," she retorted.

"Sheer determination's not always enough."

"But sometimes it is."

They walked out of the dimness of the barn into the morning sunshine and stood there looking at each other as if they'd just said something significant. Jackson had no idea what it was. Darcy's curly hair caught the sun and turned to fire.

She turned to her truck.

"I've got to have a shower," she said. "Can I borrow your bathroom, Jackson?"

He forgot all about trying to put distance between them.

"For a fee."

She opened the door and reached for a bag behind the seat.

"Take it off *my* fee," she said.

"Did I tell you I don't own that mare?"

She laughed and handed him the bag as naturally as if they were traveling together.

"I guess I'll send the bill to Blake Collier, then."

She slipped the strap of a square black cosmetic case onto her shoulder, and they walked toward the house, cozy as could be. He had no strength of character at all.

"You know, if Blake pays me, I'll have to let him have the horses," she said lightly.

They glanced at each other.

"Fat chance," they said together, wryly, smiling like two kids plotting mischief.

He held open the screen door for her. He tried not to watch her as she went ahead of him into the kitchen, but he didn't quite succeed.

"You want this in the bedroom or bathroom?" he said.

She turned and reached for the bag, but he didn't give it up. "I'll carry it."

She smiled her thanks. "Bedroom. If you've got one I can use."

"Down the hall. First door on your right."

He followed her in and put the bag on the bed.

Then he couldn't even do something so simple as turn around and walk out.

"Help yourself to anything you can find," he said. "Towels're in the box cupboard in the bathroom."

"New, fluffy ones, or are all of those at the barn?"

She turned to him with a teasing smile that sent a sharp pang of desire straight through him.

He wanted to kiss her. Even more than he'd wanted it before.

And she would probably turn her face away if he tried.

That pure fear made him step back.

"You'll have to find out for yourself," he said, as he turned to go. "I'll see about breakfast."

She unzipped the bag. "Thanks, Jackson."

"No problem."

He got out of there and closed the door behind him, then walked down the hall and into the kitchen as fast as he could. Only to stand in the middle of it trying to think what to do next.

He heard Darcy open the squeaky bedroom door, pad across the hallway—sounded like on her bare feet—and close the bathroom door. Something clunked, something rattled, then in a moment, water began to run.

Every time Darcy smiled at him, it felt like the sun shining on a rare snowfall.

Whenever she smiled at him, whatever the reason, he felt more like a man than he had since the wreck.

Absently, he walked to the stove and looked to see how the fire was doing. It needed a stick, so he put one in.

He went to the refrigerator, opened the door and stood staring at its contents.

What was it about Darcy that touched him? Maybe the fact that she had her own sadness to carry, yet she could still laugh.

Maybe the fact that she'd stopped to help a stranger. And had practically browbeaten him to make him let her do it.

He grinned at the memory.

"Aieee!"

Her scream tore through the house so suddenly he froze for a second.

"Oh, oh! Help! It's too *hot!*"

He was already moving, running with his awkward gait across the kitchen and down the hall. Dear Lord, if she'd been burned it'd be all his fault!

A whole new, terrible guilt seared a hole in his stomach as he burst into the bathroom. How stupid could he be?

The door slammed against the wall with a sharp crack.

Over that noise and the running water, he yelled, "Are you burned?"

"No, but it was close," she yelled back. "I'm scared to try to turn it off."

The flurried shape of her soft flesh against the clear plastic curtain sent a sudden heat through his blood. Relief. What he was feeling was only relief that she could move away from the steaming torrent.

But the image burned itself into his brain as he gallantly averted his eyes.

Keeping his head turned away from her, he reached in and turned the water to go into the tub, then turned it off.

He pulled back his wet glove and looked down. So did Darcy. He could feel her gaze like he could feel the stain spreading dark and hot out onto the pale leather.

He turned on his heel and got out of there.

Instinctively, in a heartbeat, he was at his refuge—the west windows beside the fireplace, staring out across the endless expanse of the ranch. He never should have brought Darcy onto the place, much less into the house.

"Jackson?"

He whirled.

Why wouldn't she stop following him? But he couldn't hold onto that quick anger.

She'd wrapped her small body in the huge, white robe his mother had hung on his bathroom door. Her mass of wet, dark curls raged in all directions, and her eyes were fixed on him.

Never moving them from his, she began walking toward him.

She came close enough for him to smell soap and shampoo and her own citrusy scent.

Then she came close enough for him to touch.

His hands hung useless at his sides.

She wouldn't let him look away while she touched him.

She reached out and laid her hand on his arm between his rolled-up sleeve and his wrist. The tips of her fingers brushed its underside with its thousand tiny scars.

Her eyes said she knew all about it. And that she knew what she was doing.

She lifted his hand and held it between them, looked down and began to peel the wet leather away from his skin. To peel it *off* his skin.

Off the heel of his hand, then the palm, then each finger, one sure inch at a time.

Off one ugly, red, welted scar at a time.

Off the crooked middle finger and the chopped-off little finger.

He wouldn't let himself look down. He steeled himself, instead, to see the pity and revulsion that would cross her face.

Then, finally, his hand was bare with hers in the palm of it, and the back of it there in all its glory for her to see. All the burn scars gleaming thick and slick and red in the sunlight and the stub of his little finger not even looking human.

God knew, he deserved far more punishment than to watch her turn away.

But she didn't.

Instead, she looked at the repulsive sight and caressed it.

The soft sensation of her gentle fingertips came

and went with the amount of feeling he had left in his skin, but inside him it kindled a glow that spread into every inch of his body.

"It must be a pain to wear these things all the time," she said.

"I don't want to scare the old ladies and little girls," he said, amazed that he could speak lightly of this most horrible bane of his life.

When, with other people, he never could speak of it at all.

She reached for his other hand in a matter-of-fact way and removed that glove, too, then tossed the wet gloves onto a chair.

Darcy tilted her head and gave him that teasing smile that never failed to lift his heart.

"Right now you only have to worry about the thirty-something women," she said, "and we admire a man who's gone through the fire."

A chain broke and fell away from around his soul.

He pulled his hand from hers, grabbed her by the shoulders, bent his head and kissed her.

Kissed her hard.

She came up on tiptoe and leaned into him, gave him the hot sweetness of her mouth without hesitation, without restraint. She kissed him back as if she meant it.

Long-forgotten happiness sang in his blood. Darcy wanted to kiss him.

His senses opened to the rough fabric of the robe and Darcy's soft, yielding flesh and fine bones beneath it, all of which he cradled in his ungloved hands. To the fresh, alluring scent that was hers alone and the delicious mouth that heated him like the sun. He could kiss her forever.

Or until she knew the truth about him.

A deep shakiness took him on the inside, like when he was stepping onto his first bronc. No way did he deserve anything special with Darcy, not even this kiss, not after what he'd done.

But he *wanted* it. He wanted far more than this with her, and that could never be unless he told her everything.

He ended the kiss as abruptly as he'd started it.

But he couldn't let her go. He wasn't strong enough to look at her without kissing her again, and he knew it.

He let his chin brush the riot of her damp curls and took a deep breath of their fragrance.

He didn't dare hold her for long. He didn't dare caress her satiny neck. He didn't dare stroke his thumb up the curve of her throat.

"Now you've got me all wet," he said, forcing his voice not to betray him as he stepped back and let her go. "Why don't I shower, too, and we'll go out for breakfast?"

Why don't we go out in public where I can't touch you again?

She glanced at herself, in his robe, and at her bare feet. A flush pinkened her cheeks before she turned away.

"I'd better get dressed."

No, don't. Wait. Kiss me again.

He bit his tongue and forced it to say something else instead.

"Stranger just ate," he called after her as she went into the hallway. "You think he and Tara'll be all right without us for a little while? Service is fast at Hugo's. We can be back in less than an hour."

She threw him a laughing glance over her shoulder.

"You're determined to get out of cooking breakfast, aren't you, Jackson?"

"You're the one who said sheer determination will get me what I want," he said, following her.

"That's not an exact quote, Jackson. Try to be more accurate."

She vanished into the bedroom and closed the door.

Then she yelled from behind it, "That's all right. You can cook supper, instead."

"Forget that," he yelled back. "Eat a lot of breakfast."

That insidious warmth spread through him again as he went into his room. Suddenly it seemed perfectly natural to have someone to joke with in the house.

To have Darcy in the house.

The thought froze his fingers while he unbuttoned his shirt.

It needn't be a problem. She wouldn't be here for

long. Besides, a little joking around would help take the edge off their worries about the horses.

All he had to do was keep it light and jokey with strictly no kissing, and everything'd be fine.

Hugo's was busy, as always, but he didn't see any vehicles in the parking lot he recognized. Good. He hated it when people tried to be friendly when all he wanted was a hot meal.

And he'd hate to have them trying to talk to Darcy and bugging her with questions about their sick animals.

His little voice of truth amended that immediately.

You'd hate to share her with anybody else.

Ridiculous. Hadn't he been the one to suggest going out?

"Here it is," he said, and cut the motor. "The famous Hugo's."

"What's the specialty that makes it famous?" Darcy said, opening her door before he could get out.

"Location," he said. "Only place to eat for miles around."

"Then we're lucky it's so close to the ranch," she said, "in case I can't *ever* get you to cook."

"Right," he said, unable to resist laying his hand on the small of her back as he opened the door to Hugo's for her. "When you finally browbeat me into kitchen duty I'll just run down here and grab some burgers."

"That's cheating."

He escorted her the whole length of the tiny building to the booth he preferred, which was the one farthest back, away from the stools at the counter and the traffic. Most of the customers sitting at the counter were men and most of them glanced curiously at Darcy as she passed. Jackson felt a quick stab of jealousy.

That was insane, almost as stupid as when he'd been jealous of Terry. Darcy was his veterinarian—and nothing more. Yet he kept his hand right where it was until she slid into her side of the booth.

Well, they were friends, too, in a way. For now. But she'd soon be gone. All he had to do was remember what a total screwup he was and he'd be glad to see her go so she wouldn't find that out.

His jaw tightened. He had no business caring what she thought of him. He *didn't* care.

The waitress appeared with the menus.

"I want two eggs over medium, home fries, a sausage patty, biscuits and sausage gravy," Darcy announced firmly. "And orange juice and coffee."

Shaking his head, Jackson looked at her. How was it she could make him smile even when he didn't want to?

"Don't you want to look at the menu?" he said.

"No. Oh," she said, "and a cinnamon roll to go."

"The usual for me," he said, as the woman wrote on her pad.

When she'd gone, Jackson leaned into the corner

and stretched out his lame leg. It came to rest against Darcy's.

"Oh. Sorry," he said, starting to move it.

She shook her head.

"No. Leave it," she said. "Rest your leg."

Then she grinned mischievously.

"Rest now because I have plans for you this afternoon."

"Like what?"

"Oh, clean my truck. Detail it. Pick Tara's stall. And, of course, cook supper. I want steak and—"

"Uh-uh. You've already ordered too much food for a woman your size. That'll be enough for today."

She made a face at him that looked like a six-year-old's. Combined with the thought of her small self and her large breakfast, it made him smile and shake his head again.

"How can you be so full of it when you've had no sleep?" he said.

"My shower gave me my second wind. I did that all the time in vet school."

Her leg warmed his, sending heat through him, unlike a six-year-old's. Exactly like a thirty-something woman's.

The thought of what she'd said brought back that moment when she'd taken off his gloves and made him feel so free.

Fear crunched his stomach. He could get used to this. He was already used to it. Never had he felt so easy and comfortable with any woman, not even before the wreck.

Well, for her sake and his, he had better get rid of that feeling. This whole deal had nowhere to go once those horses were on the mend.

One way to put a stop to it would be to tell her the truth right now.

Yeah, sure, McMahan. Why don't you do that? A loaded gun pointed at your head couldn't make you say those words out loud.

He looked at his hands and the fresh gloves he'd put on to go out in public. Darcy looked at them, too.

She didn't say a word, but he felt the need to explain—since she'd cared enough to try to help him out, that gave her a stake in this somehow.

"It's different with anybody but you," he mumbled.

"I'm glad," she said.

When he glanced up, she was looking at him with a light in her eyes.

She touched the ends of his gloved fingers with the tips of hers. The tiny embrace went through him like lightning. Her leg was still warm against his.

"It was a truck wreck?"

He nodded. "Four-door dually and seven-horse trailer versus eighteen-wheeler." A bitter, metallic taste came into his mouth.

"How long were you in the hospital?"

"Weeks. I don't recall exactly how many."

Now. Now'd be the perfect time to tell her everything and there'd be no more of this rest your leg against mine stuff. Instead, it'd be get away from me, you liar.

But his tongue froze and he couldn't say any more. No way could he douse that light in her eyes. No woman had looked at him that way since…since he couldn't remember when.

He shifted his leg away from hers and turned restlessly to signal for coffee. This was a mistake, bringing her here. This booth was more intimate than his living room—he couldn't look at anything but her.

Behind him, the front door opened and closed.

"Well, this here place shore ain't what it used to be if we have to eat with no-good, low-down horse thieves."

Blake Collier's voice boomed down the narrow length of the café.

Darcy's eyes widened, then narrowed in a furious glare that made Jackson smile even as his anger and disgust with the man flared to life.

"If only you'd already had your breakfast," he mouthed at her, "then you could whip him."

She looked surprised, then rewarded him with a conspiratorial grin that warmed him more than a touch. He moved to get up.

But a man sitting at the counter turned and stood first, leaving his empty stool whirling noisily as conversations stopped.

"Who you callin' a horse thief, Collier?" the man from the counter said.

"McMahan. I seen his truck. Where's he at?"

Jackson slid out of the booth and stood, turning to face Collier. He began walking toward his accuser—he didn't want him to come back and start insulting Darcy.

"Here I am, Collier. State your business."

"My business is my mare," he said. "My Barpassers Image mare that is in *your* barn. Which you took out of *my* barn without my permission, and I want the world to know it."

"You've come to a good place, then," Jackson said dryly. "There's enough people here to spread the word."

The man was an idiot. Jackson would not let a horse-abusing idiot draw him into a public brawl, no matter how much he despised him. Not with Darcy watching.

Not with her being the one who'd have to pick up the pieces if Collier creamed him.

They kept walking until they met in the middle of the aisle that ran between the booths. There was hardly room here to throw a punch, but Jackson widened his stance, just in case.

He waited, but the cold sweat on his forehead didn't come. The sickening dread didn't fill his stomach. Somehow Darcy and that business with the gloves had made him stronger. Even if Collier did take a swipe or two at him, he could handle it. He wasn't as crippled up as he'd been thinking.

"You're a horse thief, McMahan."

"I don't deny it," Jackson said. "I warned you twice I'd take that mare if you kept on starving her."

"I feed my horses plenty," the big man snapped. "You had no right."

That set Jackson's temper free. He tried to hold onto it.

"Anybody with an ounce of decency had a right to haul her out of that manure pile you call a barn," Jackson snapped. "You can count her ribs from a mile away."

Jackson waited. For the first time since the wreck, he felt ready to fight if he had to, and it was a heady feeling. He wouldn't disgrace himself.

But he was smarter than this clown and he might as well prove it.

"All you had to do, Blake," he said, as reasonably as he could with the anger surging through his veins, "was sell me the mare. I made you a fair offer."

"I'll sell her now. I'll take fifty thousand dollars," Collier said.

Somebody in the back of the room hooted. "Well, I reckon you would now. Wait'll we see if she dies of starvation."

Collier's cheeks reddened even more, and he threw a glance in the direction of the taunt. Evidently, he hadn't counted on public opinion going against him.

"Of course," Jackson said suddenly, as if he'd

just thought of it, "you'll have to pay that mare's veterinary bill before you can sell her to anybody."

"I didn't call no vet."

"An abused animal is a different deal. Legally."

That made Collier stop and think. He was already in legal trouble of some kind and, Jackson had heard, was going from one attorney to another, shopping for lower fees.

Jackson turned to look for Darcy. She was sitting on the edge of her seat, her eyes glued on him.

"Dr. Hart," he said, "how much do you think this man owes you?"

"It's hard to estimate so far," she said thoughtfully, "because neither patient is yet in completely stable condition. I'm thinking between fifteen hundred and two thousand, at least, before we've got them both on their feet for good."

Collier turned even redder, which Jackson would've thought impossible, and leaned to look around him at Darcy.

"You little quack! Fifteen hundred dollars!"

"That estimate's on the low side. It'll be at least that."

"I'll not pay it!"

He made as if to get past Jackson and tell her so from close range, but Jackson stepped nearer to him, blocking him.

"You don't have to pay it, Blake," he said. "Sign transfer papers instead. I always carry some in my truck."

"And you know what you can do with them," Collier roared. "Your forty-eight hours will soon be up, McMahan. Tell all them fancy Rocking M lawyers to get ready."

He glared around the room for a moment, turned on his heel and stomped out the door.

After a moment, the buzz of many conversations started up again, and Jackson turned to go to his seat.

"You the veterinarian Terry was talking about?" a male voice said. "Okay if I run my dog over to the Rocking M this afternoon?"

Jackson opened his mouth, but before he could say anything, Darcy was smiling at the guy and handling her own business.

"Sure," she said, as she slid back into the booth. "I'm always glad to get a paying customer. What's wrong with your dog?"

Jackson joined her.

"Horse stepped on 'im," the guy said.

Jackson gave him a hard look, but he didn't know him. Young guy. With a cocky smile that said he thought he was good-looking.

"Don't be in a hurry," Jackson growled. "Dr. Hart has some horses to see to."

He wanted to tell the kid not to come to the ranch at all, but Darcy smiled at him right then. He hated to make a liar out of her.

Chapter Nine

Jackson threw another unfriendly glance at the man with the hurt dog. Almost as if he were a rival of some kind. Almost as if he were…jealous? Surely not.

"No!" Darcy cried. "Oh, no, Jackson, I wasn't thinking. I'm sorry. I forgot you don't like people coming over to the ranch. I shouldn't have taken it upon myself to say yes."

He looked surprised.

"*What* are you talking about?"

"That guy. Over there. I told him to bring his hurt dog to the Rocking M. I said it because I didn't want to leave the horses long enough to go to his place, but I can tell him…"

Jackson made an impatient gesture. "No. No problem."

The waitress set their food between them while he eyed Darcy warily. Searchingly.

"Do you need money?" he said harshly.

She nearly choked on her coffee.

"Now what are *you* talking about?"

"You told the dog man you can always use a paying customer. Do you want me to pay you what I owe you now?"

He was angry. Shocked, she leaned back in her seat, ignoring the hot, good-smelling food even though she was famished.

"Why are you so angry? Are you trying to pay me off and be rid of me so strangers won't be coming to your ranch?"

It was his turn to look shocked.

"Will you *listen* to me?" he demanded. "I'm saying you'd better not be in trouble without saying so, after the help you've given me. Are you strapped for cash or not?"

Finally it all came together in her head.

He was trying to help her out. He thought she was in dire straits.

Shaking her head, she smiled. He scowled at her.

"Jackson," she said, as she forked open a biscuit and poured gravy on it, "what would I do with cash? This may be the only time I'm off the ranch for the next week."

"You could have creditors on your trail—a truck payment due, or a mortgage. Anything."

The roughness in his voice betrayed a lot of sympathy. She reached across and touched his arm.

"Thank you, Jackson," she said, her heart suddenly full of gratitude. "That is so good of you, but really, I'm fine."

She met his eyes.

"Truly, I'm not running across Texas without a destination because creditors are chasing me."

He looked at her keenly as if judging the truth of that. Finally, he growled, "All right, then."

They began to eat, mostly in silence. Darcy pondered the events of the last few minutes. Was Jackson getting attached to her in some way? Starting to depend on her?

For the horses' care, yes, he had depended on her for that from the beginning. But now he was depending on her for friendship, expecting her to share something as intimate as money problems, being willing to dent his reclusiveness even more for her sake.

And truth was, the look he'd given that young man had looked jealous. Not to mention that he'd let her take off his gloves but he wouldn't go without them in front of anyone else.

Worry stabbed her. She had started all this.

Her removing his gloves had affected him deeply—the kiss was proof of it. Maybe she shouldn't have done that.

But she had felt the most powerful leading to do it.

Lord, I did the right thing, didn't I?

He was so fragile, though, and she was meddling with his feelings. She had horned her way into his life, taken on saving the lives of his horses, ripped his protective gloves off his hands and kissed him back like her life depended on it.

She had kissed him with all the pent-up passion in her. It scared her to even think about that kiss. Here they were, two emotional wrecks, and they were about to start something they couldn't finish.

Pent-up was the key word. She'd probably felt so much from that kiss, poured so much into it, because Jackson McMahan was the only man besides her partner she'd been around for more than five minutes and spoken more than five words to since Todd had died.

She'd needed to be held in a man's arms, needed a kiss, that was why she'd felt such an inordinate desire for Jackson. It was that simple, and she'd better get that straight in her head before she caused even more damage to him and to herself.

There was no way she was able to give Jackson the support and understanding he needed. How could she, with her heart filled with fury and grief? There was no room in it for anything else.

Dear Lord, have I led him on? Or am I reading too much into all of this, imagining things? Inflating my own importance because I haven't been important to anyone for so long?

"Jackson," she said stiffly, "thanks for asking. I

only meant that I always need money. Most veterinarians do. I didn't intend to seem desperate.''

He gave her a sharp look, then an abrupt nod.

"You handled Collier really well," she said, trying to get things back on an even keel.

He shrugged. "I surprised myself that I held my temper," he said. "I guess I just didn't want to let a sorry so-and-so like him get my goat."

They both laughed.

"Maybe Sally could butt him around the barn a couple of times and get him to sign Tara over," Darcy said.

He grinned. "Maybe. We could always try it."

He held her gaze for a long minute, then she looked down and took the last sip of her coffee.

"We'd better get going," she said. "See about our horses."

She bit her tongue as they slid out of the booth. *Our.* She didn't need to think in those terms, much less talk in them.

Hugo's cinnamon rolls were so enormous that just one fit in a carryout box meant for a whole meal. Darcy carried it with both hands, but when they got to the truck, she managed to open her door and get into the high-riding four-by-four quickly, before Jackson could help her.

He couldn't touch her again, not even in the slightest way, because that'd just make her want more. Jackson needed—and deserved—somebody peaceful and strong. Somebody ready to love him. Somebody whole.

She gave a great sigh as he started the truck and drove out of the parking lot.

"What's the matter?" he asked, with that keen, sideways glance of his.

"Nothing."

He looked at the road before he pulled onto the highway, then glanced at her again.

"Really, Jackson," she said, "I'm fine."

"You ate too much," he said. "I tried to tell you not to be a pig."

She made a playful gesture, as if to hit his arm, but stopped herself.

"It takes one to know one," she said, and smiled at him before she turned and stared out the window.

All she could see, though, was his answering smile and the question in his eyes. He sensed a change in her, but he had no idea what it was.

Lord, help me not hurt him. And help me not get attached to him any more than I am. Help me heal these horses and get me out of here with both of us in as good a shape as when I came in.

He drove fast, and they didn't talk again until they reached his road and turned in.

"I know what you're thinking," she said, "that you'll get to eat half of this cinnamon roll since it's so huge, but don't get your hopes up. It smells wonderful."

He shot her that slanting, inscrutable look of his.

"Yesterday I'd've said you couldn't eat that breakfast you just tucked away and that cinnamon roll, too," he drawled. "But after what I've seen now, anything's possible."

Not anything. Some things simply are not possible.

She made herself grin at him. This was better. This was the only way to go. Just keep it light.

And keep it business.

"I hope the horses are okay," she said.

He glanced at his watch. "We haven't been gone quite an hour."

They looked toward the house and barn and saw the big white SUV parked in the turnaround.

"Bobbie Ann," Jackson said, sounding irritated and resigned at the same time.

"Well, *I'm* glad she's here," Darcy retorted. "At least now I'm assured of a decent supper!"

And less time alone with you. Maybe by the time she leaves I won't be wanting to do things like take your gloves off again. Or kiss you.

"You're getting obsessed," he growled. "Since I'm paying you half in food, I'll be in the poor-house."

"You made me nervous telling Collier he had to pay the bill," she said. "I know he won't, so I've decided to get everything I can out of you."

"Well, don't hold your breath for me detailing your truck," he said as they reached the house. "There's LydaAnn. See if you can talk her into it."

"Great! I get to meet your sisters! Or one of them, at least."

Darcy bit her tongue again. What difference did his family make to her?

LydaAnn was a young version of her mother. She was probably twenty or so, quite a lot younger than Jackson, small and blond and quick. Her smile was very much like Bobbie Ann's as she ran toward the truck. Jackson parked it and turned off the engine.

"It's about time y'all came home," she called. "We brought lunch."

She ran to Jackson's window and leaned in, her big blue eyes searching his face.

"And what else did you busybodies bring besides lunch?"

He growled at her, but he wasn't serious about it.

"Sugar," she said, "in fifty pound sacks. To try and sweeten you up."

She made a face at him and then looked at Darcy.

"Hi," she said, "while Jackson tries to think of a witty comeback, we can get acquainted. I'm LydaAnn. Welcome to the Rocking M."

"I'm Darcy. Thanks."

LydaAnn grinned mischievously.

"Or maybe I should say to Jackson's little hermitage on the Rocking M. Remember, Jackson's home is called the Hermitage, right?"

Jackson groaned and opened his door. She stepped back to let him out.

"LydaAnn, you don't have enough to do," he said. "Get out there and detail Darcy's truck."

He stepped down from the truck and walked toward the barn.

LydaAnn watched him walk away and then looked at Darcy, who was climbing out of the truck balancing her box of dessert.

"He hates it when anybody comes over here," she said, as they both started toward the back door. "Does he talk to you?"

"Sometimes," Darcy said.

And sometimes he lets me take off his gloves and he kisses me.

If she needed any more proof that she was messing with his mind, this was it.

As they walked to the house, LydaAnn openly looked Darcy over, but she tried not to be rude about it.

"Ma said you stopped on the road to help him with Tara."

Darcy opened the back door. LydaAnn took it and motioned for her to go first.

"I did," Darcy said. "I could not bear to go on past, considering how bad that mare looked."

And how good Jackson looked.

"We appreciate it," LydaAnn said. "Our vet's out of town."

"That's what Jackson said. After I threatened him with bodily harm if he didn't let me treat Tara."

LydaAnn didn't laugh, but instantly Darcy knew

that remark had sealed the deal. She was accepted. They stopped at the kitchen door and smiled at each other.

"I'm glad you're here," LydaAnn said. "We need somebody else with a sense of humor around this ranch."

They went into the kitchen. Somewhere in the back of the house, a vacuum cleaner roared.

"Ma!" LydaAnn yelled. "Darcy's here."

The machine fell silent.

Darcy set the box containing her monster dessert on the square table in the middle of the kitchen.

"Mmm, a cinnamon roll from Hugo's. I can smell it," LydaAnn said.

"I'll share."

"Maybe later," LydaAnn said, "thanks."

Bobbie Ann came in from the hallway, smiling, and gave Darcy a hug. Darcy tried not to, but she felt immediately that they'd known each other for a long, long time.

"I'm cleaning your room for you, Darcy," Bobbie Ann said. "Don't tell Jackson, and maybe he won't catch me at it."

Darcy laughed.

"All right. Does he not allow vacuuming?"

"Only if he does it, and that's a rare occurrence, let me tell you."

"I've only been in that room long enough to change clothes," Darcy said, "and I thought it was fine. You don't have to clean it for me."

"I couldn't sleep for thinking about it," Bobbie Ann said. "So you're doing me the favor by letting me do it."

Darcy laughed.

"Well, I've heard of such obsessions," she said, "but I've never had one."

"I have a dozen," Bobbie Ann said. "Now let me show you which dish is which."

She showed Darcy the new contents of the refrigerator and, on the table, an apple pie she'd made that morning.

"Try to get Jackson to eat any time you can," she said. "He's so thin and he needs things to tempt his appetite."

"He ate a good breakfast at Hugo's just now," Darcy said.

LydaAnn laughed.

"Y'all sound like you're talking about a baby," she said.

"Well," drawled a woman's husky voice from the back doorway, "we are talking about Jackson, now, aren't we?"

"Delia!" Bobbie Ann cried. "Come in here, honey, and meet Darcy."

Delia was tall and striking, with thick black hair pulled back in a pony tail and long, long legs that went on forever. She and LydaAnn were both dressed in close-fitting jeans and starched shirts, but they could not look more different.

They were alike in one thing, though. Delia was

sizing Darcy up just as her sister had done, only much more discreetly.

"Jackson was scowling like crazy when he came into the barn a minute ago," she said. "I think he suspects you may be in here cleaning the house, Mom."

"I don't care if it makes him mad or not, I was too embarrassed for Darcy to be here in the dirt," Bobbie Ann said. "I just had to do something about it."

"You just had to do *something,* you mean," her daughters chorused.

"They say I can't sit still," Bobbie Ann said, turning to Darcy, "but really, I relax all the time." She turned away. "Now, excuse me, girls. I need to finish my job."

They all laughed at that. She left them, and a little silence fell.

"I need to check the horses," Darcy said, "but I assure y'all I *can* sit still sometimes."

"You're a girl after my own heart," Delia drawled, turning to head for the barn with Darcy. "And a little dirt doesn't bother me that much, either."

The sisters walked, one on each side of her, asking questions about her and her work and Tara and Stranger, and before they even reached the sunlit yard, Darcy felt a kinship of some sort with Delia, too. She judged her to be only a year or so younger than her own twenty-seven years. She knew they were judging her, but if she had a brother like Jackson, she'd be concerned about what woman had moved onto his place, too, even if it was mostly into his barn instead of his house.

"So," she said, "tell me about yourselves. Do y'all have jobs, go to school, work on the ranch or what?"

"I'm a professional barrel racer," LydaAnn said. "And Delia is an amateur fiddler."

Delia rolled her eyes at her sister.

"Is that true?" Darcy asked, fascinated.

"Well, amateur fiddlers obviously don't make a living at it," Delia said, in her husky voice, "so I'm also breeding manager for the ranch."

She gave LydaAnn a look.

"Which is a hugely responsible, *professional* position."

LydaAnn ignored her. "And I do the PR and the ads for the ranch," she said.

"Most of which feature color photos of herself running barrels or sitting on her horse as she receives trophies and big checks," Delia said wryly.

LydaAnn was completely unperturbed. "To show what the *horses* can do," she said, grinning. "And that's not *most* of the ads. Only a few."

Everything they said was laced with an underlying affection for each other, and Darcy's eternal wish for a sister surged to life. It'd be fun to hang around the Rocking M just to talk to these two.

A warning bell rang in the back of her mind. There

was something else that'd work against her—her childhood need for a big family. That, combined with her woman's need for a man's comforting embrace, could get her into a world of hurt.

What she had to remember was that this whole deal was temporary. She'd be gone in a week or so, and all these people, including Jackson, would be memories.

But then, when she saw him, her heart beat harder in spite of all her resolute thoughts. With his hat pushed back and his chiseled profile silhouetted in the sunlight from the open window, he looked like a Remington sculpture. He was in Sally's stall.

"Think it's about time for another feeding, Doc?"

It was stupid, but she thrilled to the nickname, too.

"Wouldn't hurt to see if Stranger's hungry. He needs every drop of nourishment he can get."

She looked into the mare's stall. Stranger was nestled in his little bed of straw, his head down. Worry tugged at her. Not a particularly good sign.

LydaAnn and Delia had to see their old friend Tara and pet her, but before they went in, Jackson brought Stranger into the aisle, so as not to get him too excited or upset before he ate. He came along seeming fairly lively, and Darcy's anxiety eased a bit. Maybe she was imagining things.

Sally was just as cooperative and concerned about him as the first time she fed him. She was a natural nurse goat, taking charge of the foal as if he were her baby.

"I can't wait until Stranger grows bigger than she is," LydaAnn said, watching them over the door of the stall. "Then it's so funny to watch the goat boss the horse around."

But Stranger didn't nurse nearly as enthusiastically as he had the first time.

Nor for nearly as long a time.

He quit. Darcy tried, Jackson tried, Sally tried, but the colt refused all their urgings to take more milk.

"I don't think he even took half what he did at the first feeding, do you, Jackson?"

"No," he said tightly, stroking the colt's neck, looking at him with his face stark.

Her stomach constricted. He didn't need this. She didn't need this. She had just begun to believe that both mare and foal would be all right.

Oh, Lord, please let them be well. Don't let this baby die.

"Do you think he has septicemia?" Jackson asked in a wretched tone.

"It's too soon to tell," Darcy said. "We fed him early, remember? And decreased milk intake is the first sign of nearly any illness a foal might contract."

Jackson didn't say any more.

"Let's put him back on fluids and watch him until some more specific symptoms show us what's going on with him," she said, trying to keep the weariness out of her voice.

Lord, help me help Jackson get through this.

Which was a ridiculous prayer. Her feelings were worn thin from overuse this morning.

Jackson put Stranger in his stall and left the barn without a word to anyone. LydaAnn and Delia stared at Darcy with fear in their eyes. At that moment, different as they were, they looked exactly alike.

"Oh, Darcy," LydaAnn said. "I don't know if Jackson can take another hard blow like losing this colt."

"He's really attached to him, isn't he?" Delia said.

"Tara's a full sister to a mare named Sophy who died in the wreck with the foal at her side," LydaAnn said, her gaze still holding Darcy's.

Darcy's stomach clutched. Now she had the weight of the whole family's expectations on her shoulders, not just Jackson's.

On top of the fact that Stranger had moved right into her heart.

She was a professional. A professional who had been through a lot, and she knew how to handle adversity. She had to keep a cool head and think what to do. She had to calmly wait for symptoms and make the correct diagnosis, not let herself get overwhelmed by how much she wanted to save Jackson and his family from more sorrow.

Nor by how much she liked this mare and colt.

"Like I told Jackson," she said, trying to speak briskly in spite of the lump in her throat, "it's too soon to tell. Let's turn Sally in there with him and

Tara and see if he'll nurse again in a little while. Meantime, I'll check his mucous membranes and heart and respiration rate.''

LydaAnn and Delia helped her, Tara and Sally accepted each other right away, and Darcy did a thorough examination of the colt with no telling results.

''Often the decreased interest in eating shows up three to six hours before any other symptoms of about a dozen different foal diseases,'' she said. ''All we can do now is watch him.''

Her voice broke on the last word and she turned away to busy herself putting things into her bag. She was exhausted, that was why she felt so scattered and crazy.

This was the first time she'd felt that familiar, crushing, black despair looming over her since right before she stopped at Jackson's rig on the road. Suddenly, it was on her with a vengeance.

Her hands froze on the clasp of her bag. She'd been thinking how she couldn't help Jackson because her heart was full of bitter anger and regret. That must've brought it all to the surface again.

She couldn't breathe. She couldn't deal with this alone.

''Listen,'' she said, amazed that her voice sounded almost normal. ''Could y'all stay here, not necessarily *in* here in the stall but close enough to keep an eye on Stranger and see if he eats any more? Just for a little while?''

Delia and LydaAnn assured her that they'd be

happy to do that. Darcy left them without another word, without a backward glance. She dropped her bag onto the tack box in the aisle as she passed, and as soon as she got out of the shadowy barn, she began to run.

Straight toward the chapel sitting in all its shabby dignity in the middle of the field, its white cross gleaming.

Lord, I've got to have some help here. Please show me how to pray about this.

She didn't slacken her pace until she reached the battered double doors. As she opened them, they creaked on their hinges. Sunlight poured in and spilled down the aisle as a river of light, igniting dust motes here and there in the air. The plain altar still stood.

Slowly, she entered and walked toward it.

She was almost there, passing the first row of benches, when she realized someone was kneeling at the bench on her right. Her heart stopped. The next instant she saw it was Bobbie Ann, bent nearly double, her head in her hands.

Darcy took a deep, steadying breath. Bobbie Ann looked up, her face suffused with sorrow.

Without a word, she got to her feet then sat down. Darcy stepped around the end of the bench and sat beside her.

"Bobbie Ann," she said softly, "can I help you?"

The older woman reached over and patted her knee.

"I reckon not, sugar," she said. "But thank you for asking."

She wasn't dismissing Darcy, though. The tone of her voice was opening a conversation.

"I came here the other day," Darcy said. "Do you come often?"

"No, once in a great while. Today I just was overcome."

"I think Jackson's getting better," Darcy said, longing to comfort her.

"Well, right now it isn't Jackson," Bobbie Ann said dryly. "I've got enough troubles, I can sort of go in any direction."

Suddenly, as if realizing she was being rude not to ask, she turned to look at Darcy.

"Are you all right, honey?"

To her own shock, Darcy burst into tears. Bobbie Ann put her arms around her and let her cry on her shoulder. Finally, she lifted Darcy's head.

"That's enough, now, you'll make yourself sick," she said. "Talk to me instead."

So Darcy poured out her whole story of the past, and then her worries about the colt and Jackson's feelings about him. She didn't say, however, that she was scared Jackson was depending on her too much. Somehow, she couldn't bring herself to say that out loud.

"I can't *forgive* Todd," she said, going back to her main worry. "I can't get over that he killed our baby, and that is killing *me*."

She tightened her jaw and held in the new flood of tears that threatened.

Bobbie Ann pushed Darcy's hair from her hot face as if she were a little girl.

"What killed your son was that a tractor fell on top of him," she said. "What killed *my* son was a ruthless bandit with a gun. Such things happen in this world. Our job is to decide what we do after they happen."

"Jackson told me about John," Darcy said.

Bobbie Ann looked shocked.

"He did?"

"Yes. And Caitlin."

"That's what I mean, right there," Bobbie Ann said. "My children blame Caitlin. I've about worked my way past that."

"I don't know how," Darcy whispered. "Nothing's harder than losing a child."

Bobbie Ann looked stricken.

"That's true," she said, her voice amazingly steady. "But there're other ways to lose them. The hardest is when they're alive and won't come home."

Darcy stared at her.

"Did Jackson mention Monte?"

"No."

"He's my prodigal son I haven't seen in three years. I just saw him on TV on a rerun of the PBR while I was dusting the sitting room. That's what overwhelmed me."

Darcy patted Bobbie Ann's shoulder in sympathy. "He's a professional bull rider? That's enough reason to worry, right there."

Bobbie Ann smiled bitterly.

"Isn't it, though? But I'm trying to forgive him for putting me through this. He has no idea how much pain he's caused his mother."

Darcy couldn't think of a thing to say.

"Forgive, Darcy. That's what we have to do. When we don't we just compound all the hurt and destroy ourselves. Forgive your husband and put your mind on the living, including yourself."

"But how?" Darcy whispered.

"Through sheer force of will if you have to."

"Bobbie Ann, I do not have the strength."

"God does. He'll help you."

She touched Darcy's cheek so she'd turn and look into her eyes.

"All that's happened to you today is that the present has come blasting in on the past," she said. "You've lived in your old hurt for so long, and now, all of a sudden, you're feeling something from living right now—you're in the present, too."

"I guess."

"I *know*." Bobbie Ann smiled at her. Not a bitter smile this time, but a bright one, full of hope. "You can't live in both, Darcy. You'll have to give one of them up. You choose."

Chapter Ten

Darcy finished adjusting Stranger's IV, glanced at her watch, then leaned back against the wall of the stall and closed her eyes.

"What time is it?" Jackson said sharply.

He was getting more and more tense, and she wished she could think of another errand to send him on. He had done everything they could both think of to help as Stranger had gotten sicker and sicker, and now he was sitting on an overturned bucket, keeping vigil with his worried gaze fixed on the foal.

"Nearly two. Not even the middle of the afternoon," she said wearily, without opening her eyes. "Doesn't it seem like a week since your mom and sisters went home?"

Maybe she could distract him a little bit, get him to talk about something besides this sick baby. But instead of answering the question, he snapped at her.

"Why don't you go to the house and take a nap?"

She opened her mouth to snap back at him, then closed it, praying for patience.

"I can't leave Stranger."

"But you want to leave *me*. So go."

Her eyes flew open. *"What?"*

His blue eyes blazed at her as he got to his feet.

"You've hardly talked to me since we left Hugo's," he said coldly. "You act like I have the plague. Go on. I'll come and get you if he needs you."

He went to the stall door and slid back the bolt, stepped out of the way as he opened it. He motioned for her to go.

But she was frozen in place.

"Jackson," she said slowly, searching his face, "what in this wide world are you talking about?"

He broke eye contact then. His glance dropped to his gloved hand, fisted on top of the door.

"You've had time to think about it," he muttered.

Then he stepped through the door and closed it behind him.

She listened to those words hanging in the air. She had heard what she thought she'd heard.

"Your hands?" she cried. "I've had time to think about your *hands?*"

He threw up his head and turned, stared at her hard. Incredulously. Suspiciously. Furiously.

"What else?" he blurted. "You wouldn't be the

first to be sickened by the sight. No wonder you're standing around with your eyes closed.''

That just flew all over her.

''So you think I was lying,'' she said, grinding out the words through her teeth as she advanced on him. ''You think I'm such a low-down, shameless, lying hypocrite that I was doing nothing but acting there in your house when I took off your gloves? When I *kissed* you?''

''Oh, come on, Darcy, get real,'' he said harshly. ''You don't want me to touch you. You can't stand the sight of me.''

He put both hands on top of the door as if to hold it shut against her.

''And you think I'm standing around with my eyes closed because of the sickening sight of your hands with your gloves on?'' she said scornfully.

She stopped at the door and took hold of it while she glared into his face.

''I wondered why you were wearing those gloves again with us here alone,'' she said.

Surprise flickered in his eyes.

''You thought I wouldn't notice?'' she said sarcastically. ''Even though I'm supposedly obsessed with your hands? Well, Jackson, let me just tell you what not to do. Don't be putting any thoughts in my head or feelings in my heart because you don't have a clue what I'm thinking or feeling.''

He opened his mouth, but she didn't even pause to let him speak.

"So let me just *tell* you about my thoughts and feelings," she said, letting the waves of anger keep her on a roll. "You're the best-looking man I've ever seen in my life and I can think about your scarred hands for the *rest* of my life and still want to touch them…and touch you."

His eyes widened, and he stared at her even harder. She squeezed the top of the door until she thought her fingers would break, but she still couldn't stop her mouth.

"And I'd still want to *look* at you, too," she cried. "Every scarred-up, broken but beautiful *inch* of you."

Jackson's shocked blue gaze was searching her face. So that he'd be sure to believe her, so he'd know she wasn't lying, she stared into his eyes for as long as she could keep the tears back. When they came, she looked away.

It made her furious that she couldn't keep from crying whenever something made her really mad.

"Darcy. Look at me." His voice was hardly more than a whisper.

His fisted hand, in its glove, took hold of her chin. Slowly, gently, he turned her head.

His eyes were the deepest blue she'd ever seen.

"I'm sorry I misjudged you," he said, very low. "I'm sorry. I'm a little paranoid sometimes."

"So am I," she whispered, blinking away new tears. "I know what you mean."

His lips touched hers. Barely, like the flutter of a butterfly, soft and sweet.

And then he took his hand away and kissed her harder, melding his mouth to hers as if he'd never let it go, tracing the tip of his tongue along her lips as if staking his claim. She reached for him, stroked his face, thrust her fingers into his hair. He didn't even flinch when she knocked off his hat.

Then his hands, his bare hands, caressed her face and crept into her hair and cradled her head so he could slant his mouth across hers. She stood on tiptoe and let her arms fall around his neck to pull him closer.

But she needed to be closer still.

Without breaking the kiss, he pushed in on the unfastened door that stood between them, wanting to be closer to her, too, but he'd forgotten that it opened out. He dropped one hand away from her to pull on it, and she was leaning toward him so completely that she half-fell, half-stumbled into the aisle with the door, to the edge of it and into his arms.

His big arms folded around her, and he tightened his embrace to keep her in that warm circle. She clung to him.

She had never felt so safe, she thought, and then her mind left her completely. Only Jackson's mouth could speak to her and not with words now. Only Jackson's hands could tell her anything, and they said he wanted to hold onto her as much as she wanted to hold onto him.

She fell into his kiss like a scared child fell into a refuge and took all she could from its heat and its sweetness. It filled her heart to overflowing and made her want him to love her.

That one stray thought brought her back to herself. Love was way too much to think about when she didn't even know what choices she would make for her life or whether she could give up the past if she tried.

Finally, when all her breath was gone, she broke away. But she lingered for a moment, looking at him.

He widened his stance, as if bracing himself for something she might say. Or that he might say. But they only looked at each other, his big hands holding each side of her waist—lightly, but firmly, too.

Suddenly she realized that there was no urgency in his hands and none in the look they shared. No urgency and no demands. Here we are, their eyes told each other. Here we are.

Jackson lifted one of his broken, mended hands and ran the tip of his damaged thumb along the line of her cheekbone. Then he slid his fingers gently into her hair to cradle her head in his palm.

His eyes were deep, deep blue, and peaceful.

Then a cloud came over his face. His features hardened.

"Darcy…"

He stopped and didn't go on.

"Yes, Jackson?"

He let her go and stepped back.

"You just remember I never called you a liar," he said, instead of whatever it was that he'd meant to say.

He shaded his eyes with his lashes so she couldn't read it there, either.

Inside, she gave a little sigh of relief. This was no time to talk about anything, much less themselves. They had a sick colt to tend, and his raspy breathing was getting louder.

"*You* remember that you started this fight," she said.

And this kissing and gazing into each other's eyes. Maybe I blurted out too much about how gorgeous you are, and maybe I took off your gloves, but you've kissed me first, both times.

Her tone was light and easy, the way she wanted, but she meant it. She wouldn't take any responsibility for his feelings. She would not. She might've said a little bit too much there in the heat of the battle, about the rest of her life or something, but that was a figure of speech.

She couldn't even take responsibility for her own feelings. Not yet. Not until God gave her the strength that Bobbie Ann had promised.

Jackson wouldn't let her read his eyes but he wouldn't stop looking at her.

"I've got to see about this baby," she said, but it was still a couple more heartbeats before she could tear her gaze from his to turn away.

"I've got to check some cows down by the river," he said. "I'll not be gone long."

Darcy went into the stall and knelt beside Stranger. As she reached for his muzzle and stroked it, she noticed that her hands were trembling. Her breath came a little quick and short, too. Well, that was only further proof—if she needed it—that she was unaccustomed to being kissed, and it made her tense and overwrought.

It had nothing to do with Jackson as an individual, even if he did have a deep, dark taste like raw honey from the sourwood tree she'd climbed as a child. Even if she could fall into his deep blue eyes and drown.

She peeled back Stranger's lip and saw that his gums were pale. Every nonessential thought left her. He seemed to have a high fever, too.

His breathing was getting heavier. This baby must have an infection in his blood. Some foals developed toxic shock and died within hours after presenting these symptoms.

Dear Lord. Help me save this baby. You promised not to give us more burdens than we can bear.

As she leaped to her feet and ran to her truck for medicines for the foal's IV, she added a postscript.

Jackson really needs to keep this foal alive, Lord. Jackson needs some happiness.

She opened the box and started efficiently gathering what she wanted.

She had enough of trying to take responsibility for

Jackson's feelings. When this crisis was over, she was going to take on her own, and they would be all she could handle.

He didn't mind having her here. That's what Jackson still could not believe after all this time. Two or three days and nights—he couldn't even remember how many—before this crisis with the colt, and now the two or three more since Stranger had been so sick that he and Darcy had watched over him without leaving the place, hardly leaving the barn, and he still didn't want to be rid of her. It was incredible.

He didn't even mind it when she fell into a streak of talking and talking. She was interesting. In what she said, yes—well, not *all* of the time—but her eyes flashed, full of life, when she really got into the story she was telling, and her husky alto voice never failed to soothe something in him, somehow.

But it was also interesting that sometimes she talked a blue streak when she hadn't slept much at all and other times she didn't want to say a word. Both were usually fine with him.

Right now, though, he wished she'd talk. Stranger was really listless, and he'd been sick for days now, and all Jackson's ghosts and demons were starting to come around again.

Every time he thought about the possibility of having to bury this foal, he wanted to crawl in the hole with him. That'd probably be the only way to stop hearing the screams of the horses from the wreck.

"Talk to me, Darcy," he blurted. "Have you ever taken care of one this sick who lived?"

She finally took her eyes off Stranger and looked at Jackson. For half the night, it seemed, she'd been sitting cross-legged on the stall floor, leaning against the wall. Half of that time, she'd had her eyes closed.

Jackson had been sitting beside her ever since he got the water buckets refilled. Which showed, right there, what a pathetic mess he was, since getting up and down was something he'd never do again with an ounce of grace.

It was scary when he thought about it. It was like Darcy was a hearth where he could warm himself against the cold memories.

"I think so," she finally said, her voice huskier than usual.

She paused and cleared her throat. Was it because she hadn't spoken for a long time or because she was searching for the words to let him down easy?

Fear scratched him with sharp claws. He had to get a grip. This was a pitiful, no-name colt who'd probably never be worth the cost of his vetting. He might have weak lungs or arthritis or any number of other problems if he lived.

"I remember one baby we had at the hospital who was every bit this far gone before he began to rally," she said. "And Stranger's hung on this long. He's got heart."

"Like Tara."

But she didn't go ahead and say she thought he'd live.

Quick. He had to think of some way to get her started talking about something else so he'd stop remembering.

But then she heaved a big sigh, picked up a piece of straw to tear apart in her hands and said about the worst thing she could've said.

"LydaAnn said you lost a mare and foal much like these in the wreck you were in."

All the noises racketed louder in his head, the screams and grinding tires and breaking glass and all the rest.

He began talking fast to drown them out.

"The mare was a full sister to Tara," he said, "and she looked just like her. The foal, though, was a lot better bred than Stranger and a lot bigger and stronger. He was sorrel, though, like this one, and they both have that little star and snip."

Then he shot her a sideways glance. She looked at the piece of straw, dropped it and picked up another one. Somehow, Darcy not looking at him made him free to say more.

"So LydaAnn told you about that wreck?"

Trust his little sister to be shooting off her mouth.

She nodded. "Only that Sophy was Tara's sister. And your mom mentioned it the first time I met her. Where did it happen?"

"Seventy-five miles north of here on I-35."

He could say that. He could actually say those words.

"Where had you been?"

"To Fort Worth. To a cutting. On the way home, we picked up Sophy from being bred back."

Incredible as it was, he was talking about the wreck.

"Was it night?"

He lifted his eyes and looked out the stall window into the darkness.

"Yeah. A night about as black as this one."

But my truck had lights. And so did all the others. The road was busy that night. A black night is no excuse.

"This time of year, too?"

One little question at a time. And he was answering them.

"No. Middle of April."

But he couldn't just answer the question. He couldn't keep from adding information, as if he wanted her—needed her—to know what it was like.

"Hot as early summer," he said. "The air was like velvet."

This time he couldn't even keep the accompanying thought to himself.

"That was the weirdest thing about all the death and destruction," he blurted. "All that crunching metal and shattering glass so sharp and hard filling up such soft air pouring through the openings."

She didn't say anything, just stared at Stranger and

tore up another piece of straw. Because she didn't look at him, he could go on. It was hard to fathom, but he wanted to go on.

"That was the last thing I remembered," he said.

And then his conscience wouldn't let him rest.

He added, "For about three weeks."

When I remembered the most important thing of all.

Even his conscience wasn't strong enough to make him say that out loud.

"That was a mercy," she said. "Because your hands were burned, too, weren't they?"

"Yes."

"Were you trapped in the truck?"

"No. I was thrown clear...and so was Brent."

There. He had said the boy's name.

He thought for a second she was going to let it drop. Let him slide right back into the demons' grip.

But she didn't.

"You weren't thrown clear of the fire, though?"

"They say I burned my hands on the trailer. Trying to get the horses out."

Did I try to help Brent, too? Did I even look for him?

Darcy turned to look at him.

"On one leg."

"Hopping like a jackrabbit, according to one of the guys who stopped to help."

She stared at him for a minute, then she grinned. Her eyes sparkled in that way he liked.

"I knew you were stubborn, Jackson, but that proves it beyond a doubt."

Suddenly, his burdens felt much lighter. Would he be free if he told her everything?

Reality hit him like a fist.

If he told her everything, she sure as shooting wouldn't be smiling at him like this.

Darcy realized he'd said all he was going to say.

"Jackson," she said, "try not to blame yourself. You did everything you could, and that was far more than most people would have or could have done. Try to let it go."

He held her gaze. "You're a fine one to talk."

She glanced away guiltily, then met his eyes again.

"I'm working on it. I had a talk with your mom, and it made me feel better. Don't you agree it helps to talk sometimes?"

"Yeah. I guess."

"It's always worse when it's a young thing who dies, and you had Brent *and* the foal," she said. "If Todd had been alone in the accident I would still have been furious with him, but he was directly responsible for Danny's death, too, and that's what's made it so hard for me."

She looked at him for a long moment while her beautiful eyes filled with sorrow and rage.

"And I've been every bit as angry with myself for not protecting Danny as I have been with Todd," she said. "I'm guilty, too, and it's harder to forgive yourself than anyone else."

Don't I know it. God knows I know that, too.

"But you weren't at fault," she said innocently. "Don't blame yourself, Jackson, in any way."

Right. I won't. Only in every way there is.

It would make him feel better to tell her. It would be a lot better to tell someone and not feel like such a craven coward anymore.

Darcy would be the perfect person to tell, too. Soon she'd be gone, and he'd never see her again.

That thought sent a chill right through him.

He didn't want her to leave hating him the way she'd been hating Todd.

He didn't want her to leave.

That thought was enough to strike terror in his heart.

"You talked to Ma, huh?"

"Yes. And she said something that really stuck with me."

Suddenly he was afraid to hear it. Bobbie Ann had incredible intuition, and she had always been able to read her children's minds. Did she know? Had she guessed?

"What was it?" he said. "Wipe your feet on the porch? Feed your horses before you eat? Clean up after yourself?"

Darcy turned the full force of her big green eyes on him, and he gave up even trying to distract her.

"She said I can't live in both the present and the past. I have to choose."

He looked at her.

"The same is true for you, too, Jackson."

"Sounds simple, doesn't it?" he said wryly. "Talk about impossible."

"God will help us," Darcy said. "And that means you, too, no matter what. All you have to do is ask."

No matter what? You have no idea, Darcy girl.

"Bobbie Ann says I've just started to feel things in the present," Darcy said. "When all this time I've been existing with only feelings from the past."

His spine tingled.

"As usual, Bobbie Ann is a wise woman," he said.

"Think about it, Jackson," she said solemnly. "I am."

He stared at her. She had no clue what she was asking him to do.

"I don't like to think about it," he said.

"But you do. Way too often," she said. "I can tell."

"You're hanging around Ma too much," he said. "I can tell."

"Very funny," she said dryly.

He tore his gaze from hers and turned to Stranger again.

"We've got to save him," he said, fighting for a normal tone of voice. "We're too far in to back out now."

Those words hung in the still air of the barn for awhile, as if they were supposed to listen to them again.

"His breathing is quieter," Darcy said suddenly.

Stranger lifted his head and cocked it to look at them. His eyes looked brighter and more alert.

Darcy was at the foal's side in an instant, checking his gums, his temperature, everything about him.

"His gums are pink," she said, looking at Jackson with eyes brighter than the foal's. "I think he's turned the corner."

Jackson thought his heart would jump out of his chest.

They maintained their vigil through the two hours remaining until dawn, and Darcy was right. Stranger was definitely getting stronger by the minute.

"Let's go outside and watch the sun come up," Darcy said. "And then we might try him with Sally."

They walked out to the road and sat on the big rock by the flower bed where the turnaround started.

"Doesn't the world look different this morning?" she said. "I think I'll choose the present over the past."

For some reason, his heart soared up and then down.

He looked at her.

"Well, that was quick."

"I knew it the minute I knew Stranger would live. He wouldn't have if I hadn't stopped on the road and become your Good Samaritan. I made a difference, Jackson."

You've made a difference with me, too, but what it is, I don't know.

She looked at him very seriously as the yellow light wove into her hair and turned it redder.

"I dared to care, too," she said. "I cared about Stranger, and it's going to turn out all right."

"Thank you, Darcy."

She smiled that brilliant, million-dollar smile she used so rarely.

"You're welcome, Jackson. I was glad to do what I did. But God's the one you really need to thank."

"He doesn't want to hear from me."

"You might be surprised," she said. She narrowed her eyes and looked at him straight from between her long, dark lashes. "Think about it," she said. "We made a difference with this mare and this colt. We'll both always remember it. Do you hear me? They wouldn't have lived without us."

"I thought we'd covered that."

"What I'm telling you is *think* about it. Continually wallowing around in the past does nothing. No matter how many times we think about that horrible event, no matter how many times we go over every detail, we cannot change a thing."

He looked at her.

"So?"

"So let's forgive the dead *and* ourselves," she said. "Let's ask God for the strength to do it. All right?"

He had no power against her exhilaration, against

the light in her eyes. He knew he couldn't do what she said, but he didn't say so.

He nodded. He was tired to the bone, he was elated to the skies that there'd be no dying here today, and he was fascinated by this sweet voice in his ear.

And he was cold in his marrow because if she knew the truth about him she'd scorn him and hate him and blame him like she did Todd. He could never tell her.

Never.

Chapter Eleven

Darcy found it more than a little worrisome that it took all that night after Stranger's rally—of course, she was asleep the instant she stretched out on the bed, so that time didn't really count—and into the next morning for the other significance of Stranger's beginning recuperation to hit her. She slept late. She leaped up and into jeans and a T-shirt, grabbed some coffee that Jackson must've just made and ran toward the barn. She was awake and thinking, she really was, but mostly she was hoping Stranger was truly recovering and that Jackson had slept some on the cot. Mostly that. Mostly hope and gladness in the new day and her resolve to enjoy it and really live it.

But then she saw how the sunlight slanted across the ancient, weathered boards of the barn, making them shimmer gray-black, silver, white almost. And Jackson.

The sunlight slanted across him, too, where he leaned against the edge of the door opening and stared across the pasture. He seemed so intent that she stopped, cradling her coffee mug in both hands, and followed his gaze.

The cross shining in the sun. The ancient, faded adobe walls of the chapel. The narrow road beyond it, winding along between the hills. Nothing moved.

Jackson. In his blue chambray shirt and his jeans as perfectly worn as his barn, wrinkled from sleeping there all night.

He turned his head and transferred his stare to her. He knew she was there, the look said. And that was all right.

But was he glad she was there?

Her racketing heart demanded to know whether his was doing the same. Her suddenly weak arms held onto the glass mug with all the pathetic strength they had left in them.

Her shaky fingers traced the words Rocking M Ranch painted above the brand on the side of the mug. They searched the whole shape of the brand.

But her treacherous feet didn't even wonder. They clung to the ground and took root there.

That's when it hit her. She wanted to stay. She was supposed to go soon. If Stranger continued to get well, there was no reason for her to be here on the Rocking M, on this old corner of it that felt so much like home.

Jackson was right to take refuge here. There was no reason to ever go anyplace else, and she didn't care if she never even saw the rest of the ranch.

But her little voice of truth wouldn't hear that.

You don't need a refuge anymore, Darcy. You're leaving the past to live in the present, remember? You've made a choice.

But that wasn't the choice she wanted to be given right now.

She began to walk toward Jackson.

He'd been leaning with his lame leg bent a little, his boot heel on the wall behind him. He set it down, took a careful step, then slowly walked to meet her.

Finally, at last, he smiled, and it went right through her.

"You're lookin' mighty rested this morning, Miss Darcy," he said.

He took the coffee from her and drank from it. His fingers brushed against hers. He wasn't wearing his gloves.

"How's our baby?" she said.

"Coming on."

Happiness sang in his voice.

They walked side by side into the old barn, sitting solid as time on its limestone foundation. It wrapped around them with its motes of dust dancing in the sunlight and its smells of hay and manure and horses—living, breathing horses.

That smell was in this barn's studs and rafters, in its wood and stone. This barn had held horses for a hundred years.

This barn felt like home. She wanted to stay.

Three whole days and nights later, she still wanted to stay.

Darcy leaned on the fence beside Jackson and watched Tara and Stranger and Sally playing in the turnout pen for the first time and tried to live up to her vow to live in the present. This was a wonderful day. This day was a milestone for these horses who had so much heart. This day held the perfect weather in a big bowl of tan earth and blue sky. This day had a breeze that smelled of cedar and rain far off somewhere.

This day was to be wholly enjoyed, it was to be enough, if she was going to live up to the vow she'd made to herself and to God and to Jackson, too. She would live, not just exist in, each moment.

But she still wanted to stay. And that was why she had to leave.

Soon. Tonight. No, very early in the morning. She would fill her memory with this perfect day, she would take one more evening—for remembrance— of her and Jackson listening to music while they sat cross-legged on the wonderfully worn leather sofa, not too close together, and ate their delicious suppers that Bobbie Ann had cooked.

This would be her gift to herself from God. He

was giving her one more day here, and then she'd keep her vow and move on. He would show her which way to turn when she drove the truck to the road.

Early, early tomorrow morning.

Jackson must be expecting that. He hadn't asked her to go, true, but neither had he asked her to stay.

"He's gonna be a pistol, isn't he?" he said.

She was startled out of her thoughts. He'd been so quiet all day, and restless, too, but he hadn't seemed to want her to go away.

Now he appeared perfectly at peace, standing beside her. They both had their arms folded along the top railing of the fence. They'd pretty much kept their eyes on the horses ever since their elbows had accidentally touched. And remained touching.

Stranger was exploring the bigger world with his whole being and all his growing energy. At the moment, he was nosing at his shadow, giving a little jump at it every time it moved.

Darcy laughed.

"Yes, he is. No-name or not, you may want to keep him a stud just to put some curiosity into your bloodlines."

Jackson chuckled. "That'd do it, all right."

But she didn't turn to look at him. His skin was scorching hers, even through the sleeve of his shirt.

His scent, made of horses and leather and sweat from his morning's work—and the part of it that was Jackson, just Jackson—drifted to her on the breeze.

And she refused to move away because this was the first time they'd touched in a long time. By some sort of silent, mutual agreement they'd been avoiding it, and now she needed this desperately, even this one small thing.

To remember. After she'd turned one way or the other on that road out there.

"Your old buddy called," he said.

She whipped her head around to look at him.

"I don't have an old buddy," she said. "Much less one who knows where I am."

He grinned his mischievous grin. "Blake Collier. Remember him?"

She slapped his arm lightly, but her heart made a beat in double time.

"He's not my buddy," she said. "Is he still trying to take our—I mean these horses?"

Would there be trouble when she was gone and couldn't press her claim for payment of her fee?

"Wanted to come and see Stranger," he said. "He overheard Bobbie Ann telling somebody all about how tough a foal he is, and Collier wants to see him with his own eyes. That'll be proof that he didn't mistreat Tara as much as people are saying."

"When did he ever care what people say?"

Jackson chuckled.

"Exactly the question I put to him. He said, 'A horseman has to protect his reputation if he wants to stay in the business. Your word carries too much respect around here, and I'm trying to balance it some.' "

Darcy gave an unladylike snort. "Where does he get off calling himself a horseman?"

Jackson laughed. "I may've mentioned that to him, too."

"Jackson, what's he really up to?"

"Talking to me again. Trying to get me to repeat my offer for Tara so he can get a little cash out of the situation."

"So he's stopped threatening to take her back?"

"Yeah. He's an old miser and he may have the money to hire a lawyer but he won't."

He gave her a sideways grin.

"So you can give a little sigh of relief, Darcy. Tara and Stranger are on the Rocking M to stay."

She tilted her head and smiled at him.

"I always knew that," she said. "Blake Collier never had a chance against you."

The pride that leaped into his eyes thrilled her all through.

"Are you going to make the offer again?"

He shrugged. "For now I'm just gonna let him twist in the wind."

Darcy wanted the warm look connecting them to last forever.

But she turned to the horses. Forever wasn't an option here, and she'd best remember that.

"Sally's even funnier than Stranger," she said. "Look at her boss him around."

"And Tara," he said. "Keeping an eye on them once in awhile like Sally's the hired baby-sitter."

Maybe Jackson would stay in this talkative mood. Maybe he'd say something about the way he was feeling, or give her some clue, at least.

She jerked her mind from the brink of reliving his kisses. That was for later, much later, when the winter had come and she was lying awake in Oklahoma or Mexico or wherever. If she wasn't going to run from the past anymore, she'd have to think differently about that.

God would guide her. She'd leave that up to Him.

Today. This was her last day with Jackson.

"How many perfect days like this do you think we get in a year?" she said.

She turned her head to meet his sharp, slanting glance.

After two long heartbeats, he said, "Perfect how?"

He looked straight into her eyes while, for a long, long minute, she held her usually blunt tongue. She couldn't be the first to speak of feelings. She couldn't tell him she was leaving, either.

Tears might come. And he was more vulnerable than she. Any of that kind of talk had to come from him.

Besides, what was between them was habit, the habit of worrying over the mare and foal out there and working to save them. It was nothing but the bond of people in an emergency.

It was just that she'd gotten used to having that companionship and being here in this old, homey place, that was all she was feeling today. That and dreading going back out alone into the unknown.

But that'd be a piece of cake compared to the horror of losing her child, and she had survived that, hadn't she?

Finally, she said, "Oh, you know. We don't need parkas *or* those ball caps with the freeze packs and fans built in."

He grinned and shook his head, then looked away.

"That's what I'm gonna miss about you, Darcy," he drawled. "Nobody else puts things quite the way you do."

Her heart stopped beating. He was thinking about her leaving, too!

Was he hinting for her to go? Or was he telling the truth that he'd miss her?

"Nobody else can drink your bunkhouse coffee, either," she said, proud that she could speak, much less make a careless quip.

"I'm not *making* it for anybody else," he retorted, turning to look at her.

His bright blue look speared her soul.

I love you, Jackson.

She knew it in that moment, knew it in the marrow of her bones, knew it in her primal instincts like she'd known which road to take all the way down here from home.

* * *

Jackson turned over in bed and looked at the clock for the seventh time in ten minutes. He hit the on button, and the soft strains of music floated out from the CD player beside his bed.

He didn't want Darcy to know he was awake, so he tamped it down one more notch.

The sweet, heartfelt crying of the Texas fiddle began, and then Doug Sahm's world-weary voice joined in, both telling the sad story of a girl who would be gone the next morning and the man who was going to wake up with no one in his arms. ''Huggin' Thin Air'' was the title and the refrain.

Perfect for this particular night.

You wish. You haven't ever held her but twice and not for long either time. McMahan, you're too stupid to live. You want to be huggin' thin air for the rest of your miserable life?

He must've played this CD a dozen times since he'd heard Darcy moving around in her room. In the first song on it, it was the man who was leaving. In another, the woman was married. Looked like nobody could get together and stay together. Nobody.

McMahan, you're too cowardly to live.

But he wasn't going to think about that now. All he was going to dwell on was the words to this song and what they were telling him. He'd better know it and believe it. In the morning, Darcy would be gone.

He threw himself onto his back and let his head sink into the thin feather pillow, slammed one arm over his eyes to shut out the faint glow of the farm light coming through the window. No use. He could still see Darcy, in there moving around, getting dressed, packing her things, making everything ready to leave him.

What was *she* thinking? And what was she feeling?

Was she dreading leaving or chomping at the bit to get out of there and away from him? Was she so eager to be gone that she couldn't even sleep? Why didn't she just go?

He imagined her stealthily closing the door of her truck and driving down his road, turning onto the narrow highway and moving away from him through the dark. His blood chilled.

She had no business out in the dark by herself and none whatsoever going into Mexico. Too dangerous, too many bandits. John's death would bear witness to that.

Why, she probably never had been across the border. Most likely she didn't even speak Spanish.

Maybe what she was doing was waiting for first light so she *wouldn't* be traveling in the dark. She'd packed her few bottles and jars from the bathroom— he'd heard the clinking as she put them in that square black case. He'd heard the water running as she'd brushed her teeth. He'd listened to her pacing around for an hour, but she was quiet now.

Before that, he'd thought he heard her, but he didn't know for sure. She might have slept some. He surely hadn't.

Well, except for when he'd dozed off into that dream about kissing her. That had been enough to make him crazy.

He dropped his arm and turned his head toward the window. It was that heavy, close darkness that came just before first light. Soon it'd be sunup.

When Darcy decided to live in the present, she didn't fool around. She was moving right on, leaving her past behind, along with him and his sad tale of woe.

And what about you, Jackson? Are you never gonna move on, yourself?

He ought to get up out of this bed and go tell her right now. Tell her what really happened. Maybe he'd feel better for confessing to someone, and then she'd ride off into the sunrise and never tell anyone else.

That way, he'd never have to see the shock and disappointment in his mother's eyes.

But he'd have to see it in Darcy's, and that'd hurt just as much, if not more.

God will help us, she had said. *And that means you, too.*

And his own words, coming shortly after she'd said that, the words that had just hung in the air as if both of them were supposed to hear them twice.

We're too far in to back out now.

He had only meant that about Stranger. Nothing else.

Oh, yeah. Sure. Go ahead and fool yourself, McMahan.

She had really had a point, though. Going over and over what happened in the past didn't change one thing. Not one piddling little thing.

Darcy was right. If a person was going to take up space on this earth and use up air to breathe, he might as well make some kind of difference to somebody.

He threw back the covers and rolled out of bed, slapped his bare feet down on the boards of the floor.

For the minute it took him to jam his feet into his jeans and his boots, he really believed he'd go to her and ask her to stay. For the sixty seconds it took him to throw on his shirt and button it all the way down, he knew he could not let her go.

But then he opened the door of his room and stopped. He could not let her leave here hating him.

And he had to let her leave.

He had no chance of convincing her to stay. He could never live with himself if he didn't tell her everything, and she couldn't live with him if he did.

For one heartbeat he hesitated, looking down the hall toward Darcy's closed door. Glancing at the twisted mess of the sheets on his bed.

Then he stepped across the threshold and turned toward the blessed black night outside. It was too late to go back. He was in motion now. He had to go somewhere.

Darcy heard Jackson's uneven footsteps in the hall, and the blood stopped in her veins. Was he coming to her? Had he heard her running the water and realized she was getting ready to leave?

Would he ask her to stay? For a little longer? For forever?

Her chest got so tight she couldn't breathe. Could it, dear Lord, be possible that he loved her, too?

She leaned forward, pressed her forehead against the glass and made herself keep staring out into the night. What did she expect to see out there? Outside the glow of the farm light that showed her the white gravel of the turnaround and the old live oak tree between the house and the barn, there was only the deep blackness.

It didn't matter. It didn't matter whether she could see or touch or smell or taste—the only sense that mattered was her hearing. Jackson had come out of his room. He was walking down the hall.

In spite of her resolve, she whirled to look at her closed door. The old brass doorknob gleamed like a beacon.

She listened for his knock. For his voice.

But the sounds of Jackson's boot heels began to fade. Definitely, they were fading. Finally, the screen door to the back porch slammed.

Darcy set her jaw and forced herself to turn and look into the dark. She knew Jackson.

Even if he loved her, even if he had realized that and, by some miracle, had admitted it to himself, he wouldn't let himself tell her. He wouldn't let himself take that chance.

All she had to do was remember his imaginings after they'd come back from Hugo's that morning. His insecurities were still huge.

Maybe she should tell him she loved him. That'd be good for him to know, no matter what happened after that.

But she knew, as she had the thought, that she could never place that kind of burden on him. No matter what his feelings for her, Jackson wasn't ready to cope with such a thing as love.

She watched, but no dark shape crossed her line of sight. No tall, well-built, handsome man limped through the light falling from the high pole. He was probably going to the barn to check on the horses.

Had he heard her when she'd gone to check on them at two o'clock? Maybe that was why he hadn't gone out earlier. Or maybe he had slept all night.

Maybe he had fallen into bed and slept like the proverbial log and never given her a single thought.

Oh, sure, Darcy. Of course. With you running up and down the hallway to the barn and back and brushing your teeth and running water and packing all your stuff?

Maybe he had no clue that she was about to leave the Rocking M.

Of course he does. He's the one who brought up the subject this afternoon while you watched the horses. He's going to let you go or he would've said something else by now.

So why was she standing around peering out the window, straining her eyes to see him when she ought to be on the road? Waiting for daylight. Praying for daylight.

And then she'd be gone.

The fresh air coming in gave her hope. She pushed the old window higher and took a deep, long breath. It smelled of fall and of far distances and of cedars and pines. Far distances. She'd pray for guidance and go.

But she didn't turn to gather her things. She was waiting for daylight.

It came slowly, a shade of no color, a lightening so gradual it could hardly be real, yet suddenly she could see the fence and the horses in the big pasture. Color came in that same subtle way. Two of them were sorrel and one was gray.

It was time. No more reason to wait. No more nerve for waiting.

Darcy turned, picked up her bags, smoothed the coverlet on the bed one last time and walked out the door. It was best not to say goodbye. Best not to see Jackson again.

Best never to tell him that she loved him, even if she did love him more than she'd ever loved Todd. Maybe that was because he needed her so, and Todd had never really needed her at all.

She moved through the shadowy house with her

heart in her throat. He hadn't come in or she'd have heard him. Maybe he was still in the barn. Maybe he'd saddled a horse and gone to check his cattle.

Outside, the breeze stirred her hair and brought her strength. What was it about wind? It always brought her to life whenever she paid attention to it.

She crossed the gravel quickly, quietly. At the truck, she opened the door. Tara nickered. Once, and then again.

Darcy smiled. That mare was spoiled rotten. She'd always loved people, Jackson had said, and now she'd be wanting human companionship all the time.

Or maybe the mare knew she was leaving. Darcy had known horses that seemed to sense separation before it happened.

She threw her bags into the back seat. How could she leave without saying goodbye to those two? Whether Jackson was with them or not, for her own peace of mind she needed to make sure they were still all right.

As soon as she entered the barn, Tara saw her and subsided into a low, welcoming muttering. Stranger tried to make that noise, too.

"You're a rascal girl, did you know that?" Darcy said, walking down the aisle to where Tara was hanging her head over the door. "You're a silly, silly girl now that you're not sick anymore."

She rubbed the beautiful head, delighting in how bright Tara's big brown eyes looked, and hugged her neck before she opened the stall and went in to pet

Stranger, too. There was no sign of Jackson anywhere.

"You're my lovey, did you know that?" she said, and bent to embrace the foal while Tara nuzzled at them both.

Sally stood in the corner and eyed her solemnly.

"Don't even think it, Miss Nanny Goat," Darcy said. "I'm way too quick for you, anyhow."

A terrible wrench took hold of her heart and twisted it. Dear Lord, she felt utterly bereft to leave even Sally, much less these horses.

Much less Jackson McMahan.

How could she ever, ever do it?

She knelt and put her face against Stranger's sweet, warm neck for a minute before he skittered away. Then she stood and put both hands on Tara's.

"Keep up the good work, Mama," she said. "Be well."

But as she let herself out and looked at them one more time, she couldn't resist the temptation of at least saying his name out loud.

"Jackson will take good care of y'all," she said. "You just do what he asks you, now. Hear me?"

It felt so right on her tongue. It tasted like honey on her lips.

She thought she'd turn and go away, then, she really intended to do exactly that.

But she couldn't leave, somehow.

What she needed was to stand and look at this

mare and this foal and carry that picture away in her mind.

This is what I accomplished at the Rocking M. This is the difference I made.

She would think those exact words every time she remembered this moment.

And she could also think them when she remembered Jackson's battered hands. At least he'd had the freedom of leaving them bare when she was around. Someday he'd do it with other people, too.

Those two victories would be there every time she faced the danger of thinking about the past.

Every time she faced the horrible loneliness that was already scratching at her like a scrabbling claw.

Suddenly, she needed Jackson terribly. Just to look at one last time, as she'd done these horses.

She turned and ran toward her truck, fighting the fear.

He wasn't in the tack room. In spite of herself, she glanced in as she ran past.

Dear God, please give me strength, the strength to leave him. Give me the power to forget him.

As soon as she'd thrown herself into the seat, she started the motor. Then she slammed the door shut and the truck into gear.

It'd be a long, hard drive today because she wasn't stopping until she crossed some kind of a border.

There'd be a bad few minutes until she reached the two-lane highway. They'd be the worst. All she had to do was be strong and keep her gaze straight ahead until she got off the Rocking M. That was all.

She stomped on the gas and threw gravel as she accelerated, trying all the while not to panic. Not to think.

But she couldn't just fly on past the chapel. She simply could not. She lifted her foot, and the truck began to slow.

The sun was rising over the horizon, throwing deep pink rays into the sky and a glow over the earth. The cross caught a beam of light and reflected it as pure white.

Her gaze clung to it for a long moment, then followed the brightness down the ancient adobe wall. Her quick-beating heart went still.

The battered double doors stood open, flung wide to the world.

In the next instant, she knew. Jackson had left them that way. Jackson was inside the chapel.

She slammed on the brake and sat there, her hands trembling on the wheel.

He was trying to face his demons or he'd never have gone into the chapel. He was trying to move past his sorrow and into the present as she'd challenged him to do.

Here was something else she'd accomplished.

Or caused. What kind of hard path was this leading him down and who would be there for him the way Bobbie Ann had been there for her?

God would be, but she had needed Bobbie Ann to remind her of that.

Slowly, as if she were moving in a dream, she put the truck into Park and turned off the motor.

Jackson was in there and Jackson was half dead. She was the one who had started him coming back to life.

She could not pass him on the road.

Chapter Twelve

Jackson was done praying when he heard the truck on the road and then heard it stop, but he stayed on his knees at the altar. Tears plastered his palms to his face and dripped from between his fingers, but despite them—or because of them—he hated to get up from this place.

Telling it all to God had helped him feel peace. Telling it all to God had made him feel His love again. Telling it all to God had brought him back to his faith.

But he still hadn't told Darcy, and that's who was stopped out there on the road. He'd heard the loud thrum of the power-stroke engine when it started. He'd thought she'd be gone in that minute. Now he had another chance, if he was man enough to take it.

He wiped his sleeve across his face and got up.

Stay with me now, Lord. Help me hold on.

God had already known it all, all along. Darcy didn't know, wouldn't suspect in a million years. This was going to be the hard part.

He stayed where his weak leg could lean against the end of the altar and waited.

She appeared sooner than he'd thought possible, breathless and wind-blown in the bright sunshine that filled the open doorway. His heart clutched.

Darcy.

The light streamed in only halfway down the aisle. Her eyes had to get used to the dimness. She didn't see him yet.

The wind played in her hair and tousled it in every direction, making a frame for her face. He loved looking at her face, not only because it was beautiful but because she was always so intent on something.

Right now, he was that something.

But only until he told her everything.

She walked into the chapel and started toward him.

"Darcy," he said, loving the feel of her name on his lips.

She smiled then—a hesitant, unsure smile that charmed him.

"Are you okay?" she said.

"For now."

Her smile settled a little, then faded.

"For now is all we have. One moment at a time, remember?"

This one moment's all I have.

He wanted to walk to meet her, but his lame leg

was painfully stiff after kneeling so long, and he wasn't sure it would hold his weight.

She reached him, stood looking at him.

"I was surprised to see you're here," she said.

He grinned, in spite of the trembling nervousness growing in his gut.

"Never beat around the bush," he said. "That's Darcy."

She laughed softly and tilted her head. "Well?"

"You sound like I have to explain myself to you."

"You do."

Her steady, questioning look was irresistible. Besides, if he didn't tell her everything now, he'd hate himself even more.

"I got to thinking," he said. "If God wasn't in this, how did you and me and Tara all end up in the same spot that day with nobody else within miles?"

She nodded.

"Right. He was in it."

"So why?"

She went still as a stone. "What do you think, Jackson?"

Suddenly, the weight of the words he had to say crushed him, and his leg couldn't hold him any more.

"Sit," he said. "Let's sit down."

He made it to the front bench across from the altar. If he could make it that far, he could make it all the way.

Hang in here with me, Lord. Give me courage. You sent her to me. That much I know.

Darcy sat beside him, but at a little distance, at an angle, so she could see his face. He glimpsed that much from the corner of his eye. He couldn't look at her.

She waited.

Finally, he blurted, "God sent you here to take off my gloves."

He got up abruptly and walked away from her without even thinking about his leg. He didn't know how to begin.

This was all too heavy to lay on her with her own past so full of tragedy.

That was nothing but an excuse to try to save the light in her eyes when she looked at him.

He got to the narrow door in the western wall, turned the handle and pushed it back on its creaking hinges. Then he stepped over the sill and into the sunlight.

Darcy appeared by his side.

He couldn't turn, couldn't look at her, couldn't speak. If he had a horse within reach, he'd throw his clumsy leg over its back and ride off. God knew he couldn't talk about this. God knew he couldn't speak for Him. Where did he get off saying what God had meant?

"Only your gloves?" Darcy said.

Startled, he looked at her, and the rawhide knot that tied his tongue fell apart.

"Aren't you forgetting where you are?" he said,

unable to resist answering her irrepressible grin with one of his own.

"No," she said. "God knows what I'm thinking whether I say it or not."

She eyed him for a moment, laughter still playing over her face.

"Same goes for you, Jackson. But *I* can't read your mind. What are you trying to tell me?"

The acceptance in her eyes, the implication she'd just made and the new sun warm across his shoulders all gave him hope.

"God sent you here so I could tell someone. I was driving that night," he said, in such a rush that the words tumbled over each other. "I'm the one who killed them all."

She stared at him, stunned. His hope wavered for a minute, like the curls in her hair swayed in the wind.

He plunged on—he had to, because he could never bear to hear what she might say if she spoke.

"I didn't remember it for weeks," he said. "Not to make excuses, but I was unconscious so long and then so dazed it took forever before I knew they all thought Brent had been driving."

"That's not making excuses," she said. "That's fact."

"But I never set it straight," he said. "I could not work up my nerve. I kept telling myself it wouldn't make any difference, anyhow."

That wasn't scorn in her eyes. Or disgust. What was it?

"I thought since Brent was dead, it didn't matter."

"Another fact," she said.

Was she going to be totally neutral? Was she just going to stand back and judge him? Wasn't that what he wanted her to do?

Was she looking at him with no condemnation in her eyes? Could that possibly still be true when he was done with his story?

He tore his gaze away and stared over the familiar, rough, rolling land of the ranch. His refuge. But sometimes it wasn't enough to comfort him.

Help me, God. It's Darcy I need, and I know it now. If You sent her here, help me keep her here.

"No," he said. "It's a fact that he's dead, but not that the truth didn't matter. What about his folks? They think he killed himself and the horses and messed me all up."

She shook her head. "Jackson, you don't know that."

But he didn't want to hear that. He didn't want her jumping on his bandwagon and denying the truth any more than he wanted her condemnation. He really did want her to judge him. Fairly.

Lord, help me through this. Am I putting too much stock in her opinion?

"I know it's my fault they didn't hear the truth," he said. "How much they've grieved over it, I don't know."

"What they've grieved is the death of their child," she said. "I doubt the circumstances have mattered much."

"They did for you."

That stopped her for a minute. She turned away and dropped down to sit on the low adobe wall that ran from the door to what once had been the edge of the churchyard.

"My case was different," she said. "Brent was a grown man doing a job. He was past their protection."

God, does that make a difference?

Jackson went to sit beside her, straddling the low wall.

"Maybe that's different, maybe not," he said. "But the trouble is I can't forgive myself for being such a coward."

Finally she turned and looked at him with her eyes clear of the past once more.

"You were so weak and your body so battered, it's a miracle you could even think at all," she said. "No one could blame you for not taking on such a task that would drain your resources even more."

"But I do. I can't forgive myself, Darcy."

She held his gaze with her deep green one.

"Yes, you can. You've started already."

He shook his head.

"No. *God* has started forgiving me. I found that out a little while ago when He gave me back my faith."

"God has already forgiven you. He did it when you asked Him. And you forgave yourself when you started to talk about it."

He stared at her. Could that be true?

"Have you ever told this to anyone else?"

"No."

"Well, then. Think about *that* fact."

She laid her hand on his arm, and the shape of her fingers burned into his skin.

"Bobbie Ann spoke the truth," she said, so intensely he leaned toward her in spite of all his trying to keep his distance. "She said accidents happen in this world. My son died because a tractor fell on him, not because of something I did or didn't do."

It sounded good. He hesitated, but he refused to stop what he'd started.

"But I did cause the wreck," he said flatly. "I went to sleep."

"Maybe," Darcy said, with her voice and her eyes defending him so fiercely it sent a thrill through him in spite of his misery. "Maybe not."

"That's fact," he said. "Since you're so fond of facts."

"So what?" she cried. "You're human. You live in this world. You went to sleep. You certainly didn't do it on purpose."

"No. But I'd thought I was Superman and didn't need any sleep." He gave a bitter chuckle. "Now that I know I'm not, and I try to sleep, I can't sleep at all. Ironic, isn't it?"

"What had you been doing the night before you started home?"

Her sudden change in tone thrilled him again. There was nothing neutral about it. She really wanted to know. *Personally,* she wanted to know.

He shrugged.

"Doing Fort Worth. Hitting the clubs for the music. Talking horses and performances. Dancing a little. The usual."

She made him smile because she was silent for a minute, clearly trying hard to imagine it.

"Who with?"

That made him chuckle out loud in spite of all the trouble that had followed that night. It sent a shoot of happiness pushing its way through his heart's heavy despair.

She cared about him in some way. Did she love him?

She might stay if he asked her.

But how could he ever gather that much nerve?

Did he love her?

The thought galvanized his brain, sent it running to the present moment she was always talking about. He made an effort and remembered what she had asked him.

"A bunch of people," he said. "You don't know any of them."

"Drinking?"

"I don't. I always want my wits about me—what few I have."

"Well, then, you shouldn't feel guilty."

"Most likely I wouldn't't've still been drunk thirty-six hours later, anyway," he said wryly.

She sat up straighter, as if just realizing she'd stepped over a line she'd not intended to cross.

"Sorry," she said. "That's none of my business."

Somehow the happiness was growing in him. Totally without reason. Yet it was starting to spread into his veins.

"That never stopped you before," he said, teasing her.

"Thanks a lot, Jackson."

Her tone was sarcastic, but she was smiling.

"I can't believe you're so stubborn, Jackson," she said. "Yet haven't I had proof of it since the minute I met you?"

"*What* are you talking about?"

"How you're hanging onto the bad feelings and the sad thoughts and denying the good ones," she said.

She leaned closer to him and poked her forefinger into the center of his chest. He felt its smoothness against his skin, in the opening of his shirt where he hadn't buttoned it very high.

"Do you hear me?"

"I didn't even button my shirt I was in such a hurry to get away from the bad ones," he said defensively. "I'm not hanging onto them."

"Yeah, yeah," she said. "So, then, let them go."

"Just like that," he said sarcastically.

"You can do it if I did."

He grabbed her hand and brought it to his face, pressed her palm against his cheekbone so hard the pulse in her small wrist leaped, surging, beneath his damaged thumb. His blood instantly beat in rhythm with it, jumping in his veins. Could she be feeling this same cataclysm inside? Could she be falling into this same maelstrom of wanting?

Was he going to have to save them both and not just himself?

Her eyes, huge and deep, never left his.

Anything. Anything you need, Jackson, that's what I'll do.

And I would give anything to take you up on that. But I won't. Darcy, I can't.

A desolate moan escaped him as he closed his eyes and buried his mouth in her palm, set his lips to her sweet skin with a hunger so strong, so deep, that it hurt his heart. He could never let her go.

He was losing his mind. He'd told her his secret, and she still accepted him. She still liked him, even. They were still friends.

Dear God, I need her for more than that. No. No, forget I said that. No, I know I can't have her.

Maybe he cared for her, maybe he wanted her to stay there and not go, but that was as a friend. He didn't love her as a man loves a woman. He couldn't let himself. He *wouldn't*.

He *didn't* want her to stay—if she did, he was liable to disappoint her the very next day. He had thought she would take his secret and go, carry it off with her, he really had.

She must want to stay, though, or she wouldn't have stopped and come into the chapel. No, that didn't mean anything. She was good-hearted, she'd been concerned about him. That was all.

Yet she was caressing his hair. She was stroking his cheek. She was whispering something. His name.

"Jackson. Oh, Jackson."

He kissed her palm. He breathed in its tart sweetness and salty sweat. Breathed it in like there'd be no tomorrow.

Then he gently let go of her hand, pushed to his feet and walked away without a backward glance.

Darcy sat without moving until Jackson reached the pasture fence. She held his kiss carefully cupped in her right hand and that hand cradled in her left.

He hadn't walked toward the road. He hadn't walked toward the house. He hadn't walked to her truck or to his own and driven away, never to be seen or heard from again.

He hadn't given up, whether he knew that or not.

But given up on what? Asking her to stay? Telling her he loved her?

He did. She knew that now. The tragedy was that he knew it, too, but he wouldn't admit it—maybe not even to himself.

She waited until he leaned on the fence and some of the horses started ambling over to hang out with him. One of the sorrels, marked a little bit like Tara, and the gray.

Then, reaching deep inside for more strength than she thought she had, she turned away from the soul-melting sight of him and went inside the chapel. Slowly, she walked across the front and up the one aisle to the wide front doors and stood in the breeze that blew through the ancient place.

She could not talk about her feelings to Jackson. She would not. It would be the most grossly unfair thing she could do to both of them, because if he wasn't ready to love, she'd be much better off moving on.

Not to find someone else, though, because that would never happen. She loved Jackson more than she'd ever loved Todd, and that love had a thousand facets to it that she'd never known existed back then.

That was why she couldn't hang around here as his friend. No way would she even try to put herself through that.

She looked at her truck, sitting in the middle of the ranch road gleaming its cheerful red paint at her. That was how she planned to get to her future, which lay somewhere out there on the highway. All she had to do was walk to it, get in and turn the key.

But she couldn't move. The sunlight warmed her muscles so completely that they went weak. The wind picked up her hair and brushed a strand against her face while it whispered in her ear.

The wind wrapped her in warmth, too, and today

it calmed instead of livened her. It swirled around her one time more and then it lay, falling quiet to embrace the enduring land just as it had for untold years before. And would again.

The wind was quiet now but the murmuring went on, floating along the sunlight to surround her. The ancient spirits, all the women who had poured their lives into this place, all the men who had come there knowing it was where they would live out their years.

She let go of her breath to listen.

Old voices, ancient tones, humming in the air.

Stay. Stay.

A feeling suffused on the sunshine.

It filled her, that feeling, and she stayed still.

In a little while she would leave. She wouldn't stand here and listen and feel for Jackson to stir the air behind her for very long. She couldn't. It drained the heart out of her.

The sun was rising higher, chasing the chill from the air. It was going to be a hot one. This time of year, tomorrow could be a cold one with a norther blowing through. She ought to turn south out there on the highway.

All this time and adventure, and she felt so much better, but still she had no desire to go home. She'd had no family but Todd and Danny since she was a teenager and no true, close friends since veterinary school. Her partner was a good one, but not a friend.

Maybe the getting better and the help from Bobbie Ann were the reasons God had brought her to the

Rocking M. Maybe Jackson had nothing to do with it.

No, she'd helped Jackson, and Bobbie Ann had helped her. That was it.

Now, since she'd realized it, she'd just get her breath back for a minute and gather her wits before she started out. That'd be wise, because she was liable to be driving slightly distracted.

And drunk on this kiss she was still holding in her hand.

She was pathetic, that's all there was to it.

Something scrabbled in the ground at one corner of the church, and Darcy startled. Her insane brain jumped. *Jackson?*

No. Of course not. A roadrunner bird darted out of a mesquite bush with awe-inspiring speed and raced toward her truck. She ought to follow him.

She would if her knees hadn't gone weak. Stumbling a little, she took a couple of steps forward and sat down on the one crumbling step. A minute more. That would be all.

Yet she had been the one to start Jackson's healing, hadn't she? Shouldn't she help him continue it so his spirit could be whole again some day?

She'd stopped without being asked for help, just like the Good Samaritan on the Jericho road, and she'd stepped right into Jackson's life and his mind. Shouldn't she stay long enough to see that his healing continued, as that good man did for the poor wounded traveler he found? He hadn't had any permission or asked for any.

This was God leading her to help Jackson take one more step out of his habit of denying the truth. She would go to him and tell him that she knew he loved her, whether he was ready to admit it or not—to her or to himself. She would tell him she wasn't leaving until he looked her square in the eye and told her to get out of there.

Strength poured into her legs and arms. She stood up and turned around.

And there was Jackson, walking through the wide doorway. Coming to her.

"It's a good thing you're still here."

His voice, low and rich and sure of itself, was as warm to her blood as his kiss was in her hand.

"Why do you say that?"

"Saves me a long drive."

"To where?"

He came out of the church into the sunshine and walked to her, took her hand to pull her down to sit again as he awkwardly lowered himself to sit beside her.

He waited a second, staring at the white gravel road. He swallowed hard.

"Chasing you. Wherever you went."

He sounded sure of himself, and in a way she could feel that in him, but there was a terrible tension, too, in the way he kept looking straight ahead while he talked to her.

"And why would you be chasing me, Jackson?"

Suddenly, that just made her mad. Why'd he have to doubt himself so much? Why couldn't he face up to the fact that he loved her the way he'd faced up to the fact that he needed to tell his awful secret?

"You haven't exactly been chasing me around the haystack up to now," she said tartly.

He turned and stared at her, his blue eyes startled, then annoyed, then amused.

"I didn't know it until just now, not until I turned and looked back at this chapel and thought about how God came to me while I was on my knees in here this morning."

"Didn't know what?"

"That I couldn't let you go without telling you that you saved me, too, not just Tara and Stranger."

Her heart dropped. A little. But he wasn't finished yet. She could see something more in his eyes.

"Thank you, Jackson," she said. "That's very thoughtful of you."

She waited.

Finally, she said, "Was that the only reason you were going to chase me down the road?"

"No. I was also going to tell you that I've been trying to spare you a painful decision," he drawled, in a light tone that sounded only slightly forced. "If not for that, I'd've been chasing you all over the ranch, all this time, even if I'd had to do it on horseback.''

Her last apprehension vanished.

Hope burst into life in her heart.

She smiled at him, to give him courage.

''And what might that painful decision be, Jackson?'' she drawled back.

''Whether you'll stay here or leave here,'' he said, holding her gaze with a boldness that said he meant business.

And meant her to stay quiet until he finished what he had come to say.

''Darcy, I've decided to chase you now and I won't quit until I catch you. But first, I need to make sure you want that to happen.''

She could fall into his blue, blue eyes and stay there forever.

''Why do you think I might not?''

''Because when I catch you I intend to marry you,'' he said, still in that firm, quiet way with the watchful look. ''And that really isn't fair to you.''

''Why not? Do I not get to marry you back?''

That brought a smile peeking through his seriousness, but he turned away.

At first she thought it was so she wouldn't see it, but he gestured to his lame leg, stiff out in front of him, and then turned his hands palms down on the faded thighs of his jeans.

"It's not fair to ask a woman—especially not you—to tie her life to that of such a damaged man."

He lifted his head and stared into the far distance.

"I said that to Rhonda soon after the wreck, and she agreed with me. She broke our engagement right then."

"Stupid girl," Darcy said. "But why especially not me?"

"Because you're too generous," he said slowly, speaking directly to the sky, "and too good to try to help every hurting thing."

"Meaning what? That I might say yes out of the goodness of my heart? And not mean it?"

He turned to look at her, his eyes wide.

"No! I *know* you'd mean it. You'd stay with me even if someday you realized you didn't want to."

He swallowed hard.

"Even if somebody better came along."

Darcy looked at him as solemnly as he was looking at her, in spite of the happiness beginning to lift her spirit to the blue, blue sky that, today, was the very color of his eyes.

"Jackson," she said, "there will never be anybody better than you for me. Never. I already knew that when I got in my truck to leave."

She watched while the words settled into his heart, watched him begin to believe.

"I am curious about one thing, though, Mr. McMahan," she said. "Why is it, *exactly*, that you've decided at this late date to chase me around Texas—by truck, horseback *or* on foot?''

He took her shoulders in both his big hands and turned her to face him.

''I love you, Dr. Hart,'' he said. ''And nobody else could ever love you better.''

* * * * *

Meet Jackson's older brother, Clint,
in the next emotional book of
THE McMAHANS OF TEXAS *series,*

MIDNIGHT FAITH.

Available October 2002, only from
Steeple Hill Love Inspired.

Dear Reader,

This story of veterinarian Darcy Hart and reclusive rancher Jackson McMahan may be my very favorite of all my books. Any of us can find ourselves called by God to help a stranger who is more wounded by life than we are, and in giving that help receive love in return.

That kind of giving and receiving began on the side of a narrow Texas road the day Darcy ran away from Oklahoma, fleeing from her grief. That same early morning Jackson was compelled to rescue a neglected, pregnant mare he used to own. Once Darcy stopped to help him, their journeys would never be separate again.

While you hold *Stranger at the Crossroads* in your hands, I'm back in the Texas Hill country on the McMahan Ranch, the Rocking M, following the love stories of Jackson's brothers, Clint and Monte, to their own happy endings. I hope you will look for them, too.

Please let me know how you like this book. I would love to hear from you. You can reach me c/o Steeple Hill Books, 300 East 42nd St., New York, NY 10017.

Warm wishes,

Gena Dalton

Next Month From Steeple Hill's™

Love Inspired®

Loving Treasures
by
Gail Gaymer Martin

After her past heartache, Jemma Dupre wanted to
prove she could stand on her own. However,
Philip Somerville was nothing like her late husband.
Dependable and loving, he offered her everything she
had ever dreamed of. But could he show her that God's
plan included the treasure of a second chance at love?

**Don't miss
LOVING TREASURES**

On sale June 2002

Next Month From Steeple Hill's™

Love Inspired®
Silver Lining
by
Kate Welsh

Ross Taggert had grumpiness down to a science, but
Amelia Howard knew that God could work wonders
on even the toughest of his flock. Deep down, Ross had
faith, and a lethal charm that had Amelia hooked from
the very start. All he needed was a little love to bring
his heart out of hibernation!

**Don't miss
SILVER LINING**

On sale May 2002

Visit us at www.steeplehill.com   LISL